QUEEN AMID ASHES

ALSO BY
Christopher Ruocchio

THE SUN EATER:

EMPIRE OF SILENCE

HOWLING DARK

DEMON IN WHITE

KINGDOMS OF DEATH

ASHES OF MAN

DISQUIET GODS (COMING 2024)

THE LESSER DEVIL

THE DREGS OF EMPIRE

TALES OF THE SUN EATER, VOL. 1

TALES OF THE SUN EATER, VOL. 2

TALES OF THE SUN EATER, VOL. 3

Christopher Ruocchio

QUEEN AMID ASHES

A TALE OF THE SUN EATER

Copyright © 2024 by Ruocchio Ventures.
All Rights Reserved.

Cover Art by John Barry Ballaran.
Cover Design by Jenna Ruocchio.
Page Design by The Logical Choice.
Published through Amazon Kindle Direct Publishing.

All characters in this book are fictitious.
Any resemblance to persons living or dead is strictly coincidental.

The scanning, uploading, and distribution of this book via the Internet or any other means without the permission of the author is illegal and punishable by law. Please purchase only authorized electronic editions, and do not participate in or encourage the electronic piracy of copyrighted materials. Your support of the author's rights is appreciated.

To Erin, Libby, Heather, and Uncle Pete,
I couldn't have self-published without you.

THE SUN IS HIGH . . .
15

THE BARONESS
31

THE SATANIC MILL
49

DEATH BY WATER
67

THE SURVIVORS
89

OF FLIES AND SPIDERS
107

JUSTICE
125

THE HANGED MAN
139

THE DEVIL'S LOOKING GLASS
151

...AND THE EMPEROR IS FAR AWAY
155

HOUSE MARLOWE OF DELOS: A BRIEF HISTORY
165

THE ARCHONS OF MEIDUA PREFECTURE
193

"When, with flame all around him aspirant,
 Stood flushed, as a harp-player stands,
 The implacable beautiful tyrant,
 Rose-crowned, having death in his hands;
 And a sound as the sound of loud water
 Smote far through the flight of the fires,
 And mixed with the lightning of slaughter
 A thunder of lyres.

— A.C. Swinburne

AUTHOR'S NOTE

THERE'S A LOT OF parts about being a writer I didn't expect: the long waits between communications with editors and publishers, the long and very personal messages from people all over the world, the personal generosity of my readers... but right at the top of the list is the gratitude. I didn't expect people to *thank* me for doing my job. Now, it's a fun job—the best job in all the world—at least to my mind. Being able to entertain and distract you all from the ugliness of the world and the difficulties of life—if only for a little while—by telling nonsense stories about a future that will never be is a joy and a privilege. But it is work all the same, and I can't imagine that I would be thanked quite as effusively by my customers were I still a waiter at the Casa Carbone in Raleigh, or if I were still only a junior editor at Baen Books. We don't thank most workers near as much as we thank entertainers—though perhaps we should.

So I would like to take this introduction as an opportunity to put that gratitude back where it belongs: on you. No one can run a business without customers, and that *is* what I am: a business. Because of readers like you, I am able to provide for my small family and live a very comfortable and blessed life. So while I'm grateful for everyone's kind words over the years and humbled to have been allowed to play a small part in each of your lives, please know that each of you—my readers—has played a far larger part of mine.

None of my books (except the first, which was a pure financial gamble on the part of my publishers) would exist without you all, this book perhaps most of all. Its predecessor, *The Lesser Devil & Other Stories* was another sort of gamble, and not just for me. It was the first original book produced by Planet 9 Press and Anderida Books, and we weren't really sure how successful an experiment it would prove.

If the existence of this volume hasn't clued you in: it went very well.

The Lesser Devil & Other Stories sold out in just a couple of weeks, and when that happened, we knew we needed to do another! Here then, is that other. In this book, you'll find seven stories, all previously printed, but never before bundled together in one volume, as well as one little essay at the end that has never before been seen.

The lead novella, *Queen Amid Ashes,* follows Hadrian Marlowe in his first mission as an Imperial knight, and follows more or less directly after the ending of *Howling Dark*. It was written for an anthology called *Sword & Planet,* and appears here slightly revised and expanded, and even includes one short, all-new chapter.

The other stories appeared in various places, but most recently were printed in my ebook collection *Tales of the Sun Eater, Vol. 2,* which released in June of AD 2022. Longtime readers of the Sun Eater series will recognize some familiar faces. Hadrian himself appears again in "Knowledge," a very short piece (and a personal favorite) set between the events of *Empire of Silence* and *Howling Dark*. Valka gets a turn as the point of view character in "Good Intentions," which was actually one of the first stories I ever wrote, but which ended up stuck in development hell for years due to one failed Kickstarter magazine and another (successful) Kickstarter campaign. And the Lesser Devil himself, Lord Crispin Marlowe, returns in "The Four Devils," a novelette-sequel to *The Lesser Devil*.

Will there be a third collection like this one? I hope so! As I write these words, I have not yet written a third Sun Eater novella, and we're going to need one to tentpole a third collection. But I do have plans to write at least two more side-character novellas (one for Lorian, one for Valka), but neither of these exists just yet. I am hoping to get to work on one between the production of books six and seven, but I won't know if that will be possible for a little while yet.

In the meantime, I very much hope that you will enjoy this collection. *Queen Amid Ashes* is very special to me. I wrote it during a particularly trying period in my life, and am still surprised it exists at all. Thank you for purchasing this collection, and I hope that it occupies a place of high honor on your bookshelf, dear Reader. As I said at the top, I couldn't do any of this without each and every one of you, and I hope that Hadrian's story is only the first great adventure.

I've many more to share with you before I'm through.

—Christopher Ruocchio, August AD 2023

CHAPTER 1

THE SUN IS HIGH . . .

THE RED LIGHT of battle still scratched the sky above Thagura as the wreck of inhuman ships went to cinders in the upper airs. Each streak of light—like the mark of a claw—left its smoldering wound upon the heavens as the vessels burned and fell. The enemy had never seen us coming. For ten years the Cielcin had besieged Thagura. For ten years they had hounded its millions, hunted them for sport, gathered them into camps, into ships for transport to the fleet that had hung in orbit like a school of vampires stooping to suck the blood of the world.

We had come as fast as we could, but the space between the stars is vast, and even the fastest and the mightiest dromonds of the Imperial fleet are not enough to bridge such distances with haste. We had set out as soon as word of the attack reached us by quantum telegraph, but ships are far slower than words, and though we were victorious, it seemed a hollow victory, for we had saved little more than a desert. The locals had put up a fight, the black ruins that dotted the red world said that much at least, and in the wake of our assault we'd had reports of survivors in the hinterlands, of whole towns gone underground, retreating into the tunnels and cave warrens Thagura's first settlers had dwelt in before mankind brought air to that arid world. But of the great cites of Thagura, and of Pseldona most of all? Only bones remained.

Pseldona of the Hundred Gates! Pseldona of Many Towers! Pseldona of the Rock!

Only the Rock remained.

The Rock, and the broken fingers of those many towers strewn beneath it.

"'Tis an evil place, Hadrian," said Valka, coming to my side. She wore no armor, no uniform of Empire or our company, but dressed in her fashion after the manner of her own people: in high boots and flared trousers and the old, red leather jacket whose left sleeve—unzipped almost to the elbow—revealed the dense fractal intaglio of her Tavrosi clan *saylash*, the tattoo whose lines proclaimed her lineage to all with the wit to read it.

The winged shadows of our fliers cut the rusty soil like knives, and our own shadows mingled as she drew level with me. "No," I said, not turning to look at her. "Evil has been *done* here. It is not the same."

Would that I might have seen the city in the fullness of her flower, before the enemy came! Pseldona lay unrolled like a carpet beneath us. The ruined city yawned beneath us: a black stain upon that red world, its tumbled towers and white streets charred with plasma fire, the silicates fused to flakes of glass that crunched underfoot. The planet's earlier settlers had built their city high upon the knees of the Rock, terrace upon terrace, so that once her silver fountains and white halls had risen like the palace of some faerie queen.

Brightly painted she once had been—the queen of the cities of Thagura—her houses blue and gold and white, her banners snapping in the sirocco, and everywhere the avenues brimming with the green of date palms and olive trees.

No more.

"Where's our man?" asked Pallino, who had volunteered to captain my guard for this journey down to the surface. Unlike both Valka and me, he had donned his helmet, the faceless ivory casque of an Imperial legionnaire—albeit one crowned with the red crest of a chiliarch. He carried his energy-lance in the crook of his right arm, its bladed head swaying as he hurried ahead of the double line of our escort. "Shouldn't he be here to greet us?"

I shook my head. "They'll have seen us descend," I said, and pointed up at the ruined road that once had led to the gates of the palace atop the Rock itself. Black ruins moldered ahead and above us then, like the worn-down teeth of some chop-fallen skull. "But we're not in the palace proper yet. Malyan's people said they'd make contact nearer the crag."

"'Tis a miracle there's anyone left alive at all," said Valka, sweeping golden eyes over what remained of Pseldona.

It was her first time seeing anything of the terrors the enemy left in its wake. She had not come to the surface with me on Rustam, had not seen the black scar of the old city stretched for miles across the face of that far world, nor seen the squalor of the ship-city the survivors had built for themselves.

"But there are," I said as bracingly as I could manage.

"You heard the transmission. The Baroness herself is alive, and saved many of her people!" I hooked a thumb through my shield-belt, reassured myself that the hilt of my sword still hung proper in its clasp. It would not do to dwell upon all that was lost. We were victorious! Our fleet—and our new flagship, the *Tamerlane*—had broken their blockade in less than a standard day. After ten years of harvest and occupation, Thagura was free at last, and though there was pain and loss and tears of grief, there would soon be tears of joy and song and hope as man rebuilt. In years to come, a new city would rise from the ashes of the old, and in time, all that would remain of this destruction would be the tale of man's endurance. Old men would sit at card tables in cafes along the city's streets and speak of war to children for whom the very notion was a kind of myth. Boys would play at being Cielcin themselves, and those old men would shake their heads, knowing better, but not knowing how to teach their wisdom to those who followed on.

But I gave little thought to such things, then, and clapped Pallino on the shoulder. "Let's move!" I said and, raising my voice, addressed all the men of my guard. "Eyes forward, lads! Let's make a proper show for the Baroness! Let her know we're here!"

As one, my guards shifted their lances, the ceramic bayonets flashing in the red light of Thagura's sun. Gone were the red ceramics of our old uniform, the black tunics and blocky, foreign style of armor. My Red Company had been utterly transformed. What had begun as a mercenary outfit half my life before had been transmuted into an Imperial force. The brand with which the Emperor had anointed me and made me his knight still seemed to rest upon my shoulder, and the touch of it upon my brow still burned like the touch of one of the seraphim of old.

I was a knight of the Empire, no longer a rebel, no longer an outcaste, no longer a boy.

Nearly half my life I had quested for peace and for Vorgossos.

I had found Vorgossos only.

The Rock loomed above us. A great red dome of the living stone that towered thousands of feet above the sands of the Tagurine Erg. The Rock and the palace that crowned it had served House Malyan for generations, and though the palace was gone, the faces carved upon the face of the Rock remained. Thagura had been settled thousands of years before, and the nobiles who ruled over it had carved their likenesses a thousand feet high into the walls beneath the blasted crown. The relief images of Baron Aram Malyan—who raised up the city—and his son, Vahan, stood to either side of the rising path, their hands supporting the rim of the acropolis, their muscled bodies seeming to support the palace their family called home.

I had seen them from the fliers as we approached, but seeing them then, from the ground . . . It was a humbling experience. I was overawed. I had already traveled far in my forty years, had plumbed the depths of Vorgossos and knelt before Caesar himself in the Georgian Chapel of the Peronine Palace on Forum, but there is no shortage of wonders in creation, and the twin colossi carved into the face of the Rock were mighty indeed. How many hands had labored there, and for how many decades?

Still they had not fallen, though the palace above them

was dust.

"Oro, sound the horn!" I called to the herald as we mounted the steps to the plaza that stretched beneath the feet of the colossi. Shattered masonry lay all around, and the lesser statues in the dry fountain lay broken. Old blood stained the tiles, and everywhere the signs of old violence glowed white hot for those with eyes to read.

The herald sounded his clarion, and the bright noise of that trumpet echoed and died on the breeze. There was nothing. No one.

"Black planet!" Pallino cursed. "It's quiet."

"There's nothing left," Valka agreed, and drew close beside me. "There aren't even birds. Do you see?"

She was right. We might have stood upon the surface of an airless, desert moon. A tall banner—a hundred feet high—swayed from one iron pillar at the corner of the square. White with three blue lions, the banner of House Malyan. All the world was still.

"Oro, again," I said.

Again the trumpet sounded.

Bang!

A bolt of violet light struck the tiles of the square not a dozen feet from where I stood, and the trumpet blast died at once, choked off. My men reacted at once, swinging their lances from their parade holds to readiness as they crouched and searched for targets. I stepped forward, one hand slipping to the hilt of my unkindled sword while the other thumbed my shield. The static crackle of the energy curtain flickered about me, and I shifted to better place myself between Valka and our attackers.

QUEEN AMID ASHES

"Hold your fire!" I shouted, and raised a hand.

It was the bolt of an energy-lance that had struck the tiles. The Cielcin did not use such lances. Preferring to fight with scimitar and claw and the flying snakes that chewed men's flesh and slavered blood as they flew from target to target.

"Show yourselves!" I called. "We are men like you!"

"If your herald blasts his horn again, we'll shoot him dead!" came a rough voice from the roof of the crumbled building that lined the far side of the square. "There may still be Pale about!"

Both hands raised then and visible, I stepped forward, black cloak snapping about my armored shoulders. "Look above you, friend! The battle is done!" I gestured—not unlike the colossi graven above us all—until I felt as though I held the burning heavens above me. "I am Lord Hadrian Marlowe, Knight-Victorian of the Empire. We have a gift for the Baroness."

"A gift?" the man repeated.

"I come to give her back her world!" I shouted. "Were you not told? The siege is lifted! I say again: the battle is done!"

In the silence that followed, Pallino muttered, "Bit slow, aren't they?"

A man stepped out from the shadow of a second-story arch upon the balcony of the building ahead. He wore a dun greatcoat over his scratched white armor, but his bald head was bare, and though he wore a plasma rifle on a strap over one shoulder, he raised his hands to mirror mine. "Her ladyship said . . . but I did not dare believe!" The relief in his tone had an almost physical weight. "Ten years . . . is it really over?"

"I have orders from the Emperor and Lord Titus Hauptmann to bring your Baroness back to Marinus with me!" I said by way of answer. "She must give her account of all that happened here to the Strategos, that he might determine what may be done to restore your world."

The man shook his head, though whether in negation or disbelief I could not say. He rested one hand on the wall beside him, sagged as a man who has relieved himself of a terrible weight. Presently he shook himself. "Stand down, you men!" he said, and vanished within. From the ruined buildings all around, I felt more than heard the shifting of boots and swish of cloaks as men relaxed. My own men did likewise, settling back to rest.

A moment later, the bald captain emerged from the shadows of the lower door, the tails of his coat flapping on the wind. Half a dozen men filtered out behind him, sans order, each man's expression more hollow-eyed and hangdog than the last. The captain saluted, fist to breast as he bowed slightly. "I can't believe it."

"Were you not sent to greet us?"

"We were, aye, but still . . ." His eyes flickered to Valka standing at my side, and I knew how out of place she must look to him. A Tavrosi witch, golden-eyed, raven-haired and tattooed, the shoulder of her red jacket black-feathered, her whole aspect almost as foreign as the xenobites who had burned his world. "We've been trapped ten years, lordship. You're certain the Pale have gone?"

I was growing tired of the man's disbelief. "What's your name, soldier?"

Coming back to himself, the fellow saluted again, fixed his

eyes on a point over my shoulder. "Maro, sir. Vahan Maro. Captain of the lady's guard . . ." At this, he glanced around, taking in the haggard collection at his back. "What's left of it, at any rate."

Vahan, I thought, glancing up at the colossus on the left, *like the old baron.*

I extended my hand. Maro looked at me a moment, surprised to find a lord of the Imperium offering his hand like a common soldier. He took it only apprehensively. "Good to meet you, captain," I said, and nodded in a way that said we should proceed. "I am Hadrian Marlowe, as I say. This is my," I stumbled, about to say the word *paramour* as I turned to gesture at Valka, and while it was so, I was not sure how she would take the label, and so said, "*companion.* Valka Onderra of the Tavrosi."

The man's eyes widened. "A witch?"

"A doctor," she said icily, using the Tavrosi word. *Vechsrei.*

I translated for the perplexed captain, and waved him forward. "Lead the way, Maro."

They kept looking at the sky. I have never forgotten that. Every dozen or so steps, either Maro or one of his men would stop and glance up at the clouds where the Cielcin fleet fell burning and lit the sky like so many paper prayer lanterns. Step by dozen steps, Maro and his men led us toward the foot of Aram's colossus, where I spied the huge lifts that ran up behind the statue to the top of the Rock. They were ruined, but we did not make for them in any case. Instead we circled the inselberg and descended along a paved street where the barracks of the city guard stood carved into the very foundation of the Rock along our left. The invaders had carved the round symbols of their speech into the stones with claws or the points of knives. Windows stood smashed, doors staved in.

There were no bodies. Not anymore.

"Lower city's worse," Maro said. "They burned the palace, but that was after they landed and broke through our defense. They bombed the city. Firebombed it. Plasma. Scorched the whole damn thing once they'd got all they were getting from it."

"What of the rest of the planet?" Valka asked, hurrying along beside me.

Maro shook his head, but did not break stride. "We know they hit the other cities. Aramsa. Tagur. Port Reach . . . but we lost all contact early on. The Cielcin tore down the satellite grid, and what hardlines we had they cut before the first year was out. We had the telegraph—that's how we got to you—but we can't raise anyone here on the planet. We could be all there is, for all we know."

Pallino cursed.

Raising a hand for quiet, I said, "There were more than forty million people on Thagura by your own census, captain. They cannot all be gone."

The captain shrugged. Up ahead on the left, the squarish shapes of the barracks buildings gave way, allowing for channels between them that pierced the stone of the Rock like blind alleys, creating narrow streets that led up and down steps to hidden chambers within that lonely mountain.

QUEEN AMID ASHES

The heavy metal door of some hangar or garage stood shut and scarred on the main avenue, and further on I saw the thin shape of spears hammered into the earth at irregular intervals. Green banners—tattered and long faded—flapped there, each tall almost as I was and thin. They were not the banners of House Malyan, and at this distance I could not read the alien ruins painted or embroidered on them, but I knew the skulls that decorated their posts were those of men.

The tired captain stopped before one of the narrow alleyways and turned to face me. "I pray you may be right, lordship. Earth knows, I pray. But ten years is a long time. Maybe some of the desert folk got away, or some of the archons and their families survived in other bunkers, but the cities?" He only shook his head, and rubbing his bald scalp with a gauntleted hand, he turned and gestured down the passage. "It's this way."

The great lords of the Imperium had been digging tunnels since the days of the God Emperor. The dangers of interhouse warfare were never zero, and shielded or no, the great palaces and estates of the various barons, counts, dukes, and marquises were ever targets for orbital bombardment, whatever the Great Charter and the formal rules of war may say. There was hardly a palace beneath any of the Sollan Empire's half a billion suns that did not possess something like the bunkers in which Gadar Malyan and her court found herself. Some planets and castles possessed only the most rudimentary of boltholes—sufficient to sustain a lesser lord, his family, and a scarce dozen or more retainers—while others boasted a complex warren of tunnels from which a planet's resistance might be directed. Still others were the palaces themselves, whole halls and galleries resided in darkness below the earth.

They were relics of an older time, when man battled man for honor and for gain. How prescient that need had been, and how fortunate. In preparing to battle ourselves, we had prepared for the invaders, for the Cielcin to sweep in from galactic north and lay waste to our many worlds.

Valka and I turned down the narrow alleyway, Pallino and the men of our guard behind. Three of Maro's men hurried on ahead, headlamps illuminating the path as they reached the top of a winding stair that angled down. At the bottom, a pair of men in tan cloaks like Maro's greeted us with curt nods, and from the way they saluted Maro, I guessed they'd been left to hold the garret. The room itself was dark, and from what little I saw, I guessed it had been an intake chamber of the sort one finds in the offices of urban prefects under every sun. It was not hard to imagine criminals dragged off the streets of Pseldona and hauled in to explain themselves to a prefect before being dragged down to lockup. I spied reinforced glass on the inner doors, and empty lockers—their doors twisted and strewn about the place—where once the effects of detainees were kept.

"The entrance to the bunker is through the dungeons?" I asked, somewhat surprised.

"No," Maro answered. "Through the castellan's offices. Through here." He gestured, then turned back to his men. "Tilcho, Garan, you two stay here until my signal. It's quiet out there, but that doesn't mean we haven't been followed."

"Aye, sir."

Once we passed through the intake chamber, we followed

Maro's men along the ruined hall. It seemed there was nowhere the xenobites had not gotten, for here too were signs of looting and more rude graffiti.

When we hurried down another three levels by a spiral flight of stairs, Maro asked, "Is it true, lordship? What they say of you?"

I had passed Maro then, and flinched as though the man had rammed a dagger between my shoulder blades. Had the story reached even here?

Is it true you can't be killed?

Valka's golden eyes—artificial as they were, confections of metal and glass—glowed at me in the dimness, her face opened in concern. She had been there, had seen me die, had screamed as the inhuman Prince Aranata's blade struck off my head. As had Pallino and a number of my guard. The story had begun to get out: How I had simply *appeared* again, alive. How I had saved Valka and my people from the prince at the last moment.

To think the story had come as far as Thagura... whispered from soldier to soldier as the Legions traveled between the stars.

No blade can cut the Devil down, they said.

But Maro did not ask the dreadful question. Instead he said, "Did you really kill one of their princes in single combat? The Cielcin, I mean."

I felt my shoulders relax and smiled. Valka smiled too and turned away. "Don't believe everything you hear, captain," I said, smiling after her and glancing at Pallino, who had fought by my side. "I had help."

"But you did kill one?"

"Aranata Otiolo," I said, thoughts running back to that

monstrous prince. Nearly eight feet tall and thin as Death, but broad-shouldered, with arms that reached its knees and horns long as daggers above its broad, white face. "Yes."

The men about us whispered in surprise and admiration. In all the centuries of war between our two kinds, I was the first—the very first—to kill one of their princes face-to-face. Titus Hauptmann, Cassian Powers—the great heroes of the early Crusade—these had killed princes by the dozen, whole blood-clans, but they had done so with the fire of their guns, with atomics and armadas to outgun the sun itself for firepower. I alone had met such a lord of demons sword for sword.

I had lost.

And lived only because *they* had brought me back. The Quiet. The ancient beings whose ghosts I first encountered in the ruins on Emesh. They had handed me back my life, and I didn't even know why.

Maro's mouth hung open, surprised to hear the answer he'd expected. "And the one that attacked us here?"

I shook my head. "Escaped to warp before we could engage."

The great worldship that housed the vast majority of the Cielcin presence at Thagura had been far out beyond the planet's moons, where it could be assured of a stable orbit and not risk destabilizing those moons with its own near-planetary bulk. We had come in hard and fast, and burned the battleships and little raiding vessels that accosted the planet itself. By the time Ramsundar Glass and the other captains made for the alien moon, the vast worldship's engines—great as empires—had blazed bright as suns.

QUEEN AMID ASHES

Briefly—too briefly—I had spoken with their prince, Inumjazi Muzugara, had ordered the chieftain to surrender. I had given it my name, told it that I had killed Otiolo, its kinsman... but it had fled. Muzugara took its whole world away at speeds faster than light, abandoning its dying fleet in the skies above Thagura.

I did not know it then, but I had planted a seed in that moment. Inumjazi Muzugara would carry my name and the tale of my deeds back to its people, and as there were stories of me told then across the Empire, there would be stories told of me among the Cielcin ere long.

"I see," said Maro, his rough voice bringing me back to the moment. "I see. We're through here, lordship."

The castellan's desk had been overturned, lay broken on the moldering carpet. A portrait of His Imperial Radiance, the Emperor William XXIII, hung slashed on one wall. Still, I recognized the green eyes and fiery red hair of the man who had knighted me. The same portrait hung duplicated in ten billion offices on a hundred million worlds. Torn books littered the ground, and smashed bits of quartz that had once held all manner of data.

One of Maro's men circled the perimeter of the room, admiring the destruction. He made a warding gesture with both hands, first and last fingers extended to ward off evil. "Black planet, they got close."

"But they didn't find the door," Maro said, unslinging his rifle. He pounded the butt of the weapon on the floor once, twice, three times. "Ciprian! Open the gate!"

A deep *click* resounded through the low, stone room, and an instant later the floor began to shake, and a terrible grinding filled the air and set my teeth on edge. A slit opened in the floor beneath where the desk had been, and two of Maro's men hurried to fold back the rug to keep it from sagging into the fresh opening. Yellow sconces flickered to life, and a dirt-faced boy in ill-fitting white armor peered up at us from the bottom of the stairs.

"Is *he* the knight?" the boy asked, eyes wide as he looked at me.

"He is," I said.

"You've come to save us!" he exclaimed. I guessed he must be Ciprian. "And the lady?"

I nodded, and looked to Maro.

The captain extended a hand. "After you."

CHAPTER 2

THE BARONESS

THUS I BRING YOU, Reader, through that hidden gate. Many times I would enter the underworld in our long war, and many times come to some catacomb, some deep-delved place dark and dank and stinking of desperation and unwashed men.

Many times.

But Thagura was the first. Though I had fought before—on Vorgossos, on Emesh—I had never come to so formal a theater of war. Our fight against Aranata beyond Vorgossos had not been planned; and on Emesh the enemy had surprised us, falling like fire from the sky. The Emperor had anointed me, created me as a knight, and though I chafed in my new station, I wore it proudly as I could. Thagura would anoint me again, a second baptism, one greater than the first. How many times would I stand in so dark a tunnel in the decades to come? On how many worlds?

I can name them all now, though as I followed the unwashed Ciprian I still believed I might count my battles on my fingers. I still hoped for peace, though I no longer knew how to achieve it. The boy who dreamed of peace on Delos long ago was dead, indeed, and though I bore his name and blood alike, I was not him. With every threshold we cross we become someone new, for every place is new, and every hour, and with every moment we are changed.

We may not step in the same river twice, nor with the same feet.

And I had stepped into the last redoubt of House Malyan upon Thagura, and doing so became a *hero*. The gallant rescuer, though it had been Captain Corvo and my officers who broke the siege in orbit, and not *Lord Hadrian Marlowe*. Gone was the boy—I say again—and in his place there strode a knight, young and tall and clad in black: black of hair and cloak, his knife-edged face so pale it seemed to glow in the dimness, his witch-companion at his side.

"They're here!" I heard a hoarse voice whisper, and saw a haggard face peer out at us from a side passage. "They're really here!"

"Is it really over?" asked an old woman in the pale smock of a nurse, appearing in yet another open door.

More faces flowered from doors left and right. Dark shadows showed beneath every eye, and all bore the gray pallor of men long-starved for light of sun. Many wore the humble suits of serving men or the dark gowns of maidservants, but there were those dressed in rumpled silks and velvet jackets, men in wigs and powdered faces, women hastily painted and untidily coiffured by tired hands to greet the heroes of the day. I raised fingers to my brow in recognition of their bows and curtsies. These were the vestiges of the Thaguran court. Survivors of the assault that burned the city and took the palace. Among them, I guessed, were the scions of the planet's lesser houses, perhaps an exsul archon or two in from mining colonies on the border of the system.

Life in the hypogeum ill-suited them, for there was a shabbiness about them all, a hunger and an exhaustion of spirit of the sort one sees in prisoners. But they *were* prisoners, had been prisoners for long years. I studied the back of young Ciprian's head. The boy could not be much older than ten—if indeed ten he was. Had he ever known the light of sun? If he had, did he remember it?

"Black planet," Pallino grumbled in my ear, "what a rotten place."

"Everybody stand clear!" exclaimed Captain Maro, raising his hands as he went on ahead of me. "He's here to see the Baroness, not you! Stand clear!" The faces in the doors and side halls drew back a pace, but their whispering and nervous motion did not abate. Apparently satisfied, Maro turned back to me and spoke from one corner of his mouth. "Pay them no mind, lordship! It's been years since any of us saw a new and friendly face. My lady awaits you in her chambers. This way!" He gestured along the main hall, straight as a die. I made to follow him.

But before I could go another three paces, a young woman broke from one of the side passages and fell to her knees before Valka and me. She seized my ankle with small, strong hands and kissed my polished boot. "Lord!" she cried, and looked up at me with shining eyes. "Earth bless and keep you, lord! Is it done? Are they gone? Is it over at last?"

At a sign from Maro, two of the Malyan soldiers seized

the woman roughly by her shoulders and hauled her to her feet. "Get back, you!" one said, shoving her whence she had come.

"Hadrian!" Valka's hand settled on my arm.

"Stand down, you men!" I exclaimed. "Leave her!"

The soldiers let her stagger against the wall. Two maidservants like herself in black gowns steadied her and looked on with hard eyes.

Maro advanced, breath on my ear as he explained, "They were ordered not to speak to you, lordship."

Taking him to mean this order had been intended as a courtesy for me, I said, "It's all right." I placed a hand on the captain's shoulder. "They've done no harm." The serving woman peered up at me, one dark eye still luminous from behind her curtain of unwashed yellow hair.

"We mustn't leave my lady waiting!" Maro said. "Come, lordship!"

Valka's shadow moved on the wall as she shifted at my side. She did not speak, but her presence was sharp enough a goad. Ignoring the captain, I went to the serving woman and took her by the shoulder, helping her still half-petrified companions to set her upright. "Are you all right?" I asked.

She nodded. I tried to smile, knowing the expression was cold comfort coming from my satyr's pointed face. Brushing back my fall of black hair, I said, "It *is* over. The enemy has gone." I released her shoulder and, turning, raised my voice so all the gathered servants and lesser courtiers might hear me. "We have driven the Pale back into the outer Dark! Their worldship fled, and their fleet is burning now all across your skies!"

QUEEN AMID ASHES

It was as if a dam had broken, as if some taut, invisible net were cut and loosed a shoal of breaths from so many tortured lungs. The woman broke down and buried her face in her hands, her shoulders heaving. Her two companions—weeping themselves—tried gently to drag her, sobbing, away. Still others cheered, and someone clapped me on the back.

"Stand down, you all!" Maro barked, stepping toward me. "Lordship! Come!" Something in the captain's voice cracked. I should have marked it then and wondered, or noticed the tension in his men, the way they bristled as the crowd clapped and cried aloud in joy and disbelief, but it was lost in the moment for me.

Turning to Maro, I nodded and ducked my head. "Lead on, then, captain."

There was a guard posted at the door to the Baroness's chambers: four shielded hoplites in the colors of House Malyan, their faces hidden behind plates of azure ceramic, their pauldrons fashioned in the shapes of snarling lions. They stood aside as Maro approached, and the door behind them slid aside. It vanished into a slot in the wall, rolling on huge gear teeth to admit us.

"Your men will wait here," said Maro, gesturing to a guardroom to the right of the main door.

"They will *not*," Pallino said stepping forward, his chin thrust out.

Addressing Pallino directly, Captain Maro said, "The Baroness has ordained that this should be a private audience."

Pallino did not move. He might have been a statue, a suit of armor on display, a carved chessman daring his opponent to move.

Captain Maro blinked. "But *you* may accompany your master, if the rest of your guards remain in the guardroom."

"That's acceptable," Pallino said, and offered the man his left hand as was the custom between soldiers of separate armies.

Amusement flickered in the corner of Valka's eyes as we crossed the threshold, Maro ahead, Pallino behind.

Gone at once were the drab walls of painted stone, the floors of scuffed, smooth concrete. Gone were the ducts and stripes of wire mold bracketed to the cracked arch of the ceiling. Gone were the open metal doors and the unwashed faces of courtiers and serving men. Tavrosi carpets lay thickly on the floor before us, and the walls glimmered with minute tilework. A dozen mosaicists must have labored for many months to decorate the walls of that atrium with mandalas and the figures of men and starships blue and white and violet, black and gold, with here and there a spark of red glass tesserae bright as gems.

A flight of stairs as ornately tiled went down straight ahead, oiled balustrades to either hand, sconces gleaming in recesses where the busts of generations past were carved. As we went down, the rippling glow of light upon water filtered up and caught on the mosaic work that lined the walls of the stairway and wrapped overhead. So beautiful was it all—and such a contrast with the drab quarters beyond the rolling door—that my breath caught.

It was as if we were descending from the mortal world to the Mag Mell where dwelt some queen of the Fae. I felt almost like a man in dream. In reality, we were only descending to a level of the bunkers deeper still, ensuring greater security cubit by cubit.

His hand steadying his rifle on its sling, Maro hurried down the stairs ahead of us. Valka and I followed him more slowly, our boots ringing as we descended into the central chamber, where a long, narrow pool of clear water shimmered in a marble basin between graven caryatids whose crowned heads upheld the living stone of the roof.

"What the hell is all this?" Valka hissed, speaking her native Tavrosi Panthai so Maro might not understand.

I could only shake my head. What compulsion had seized the lords of House Malyan and convinced them of the need for such luxury in their underground shelter I could not say. Gold and porphyry gleamed in the crowns of the caryatids, and in their pedestals, and gold banded their graceful arms. More mosaics gleamed in wall niches, displaying the heroes and worthies of our Imperial past. I recognized Prince Cyrus the Golden, the naked Amana in his arms; and there was Simeon dressed in red, the Irchtani about him! I spied the God Emperor, holding the Earth in one hand as he smashed the machines—an unmarked white cube—beneath his booted heel. More there were I did not know on sight, local heroes, perhaps.

I would have liked time to examine these great works of art, but time pressed, and Maro led us around the right edge of the great pool and up a short flight of white steps to a balcony where the water-shaped wall of a cavern ran down, ribbed pillars of limestone and stalactites concealing glowspheres and soft lamps. A rail along the inner wall overlooked the pool. The only sign that not all was as it should be were the plantings. A potted orange tree stood by the rail, long withered, and stone planters that must once have been verdurous and thick with blossom were now choked and withered with neglect.

"This is him?" a husky, richly accented voice wafted from a divan to greet us. "Enough, Ravi! Our hero is here!"

That the woman who rose from her cushioned seat was of the highest Imperial blood no man could deny. The porphyrogeneticists of the High College who had sculpted her from the blood of her parents had lavished every art upon her, for she was perfect as any of the graceful caryatids that upheld the roof of the grotto—and nearly as naked. Her eyes were twin chips of black jade, and her hair fell in curling waves of India ink—dark even as my own. As she sat up, she rearranged the translucent black silks that draped her callipygian figure like the shadows of evening, revealing the creamy flesh beneath.

With delicate care, the Baroness perched herself on the edge of her divan and extended a hand that glittered with onyx and lapis lazuli. Matching lapis enamel coated each taloned nail, and lapis, too, shone on golden chains about her bare, white throat.

I simply stood there a moment, aware that I was staring, stunned by this display and by our circumstances. Of all the ways she might have chosen to greet us . . . this?

Remembering himself a fraction too late, the woman's cup bearer—a nobile boy of perhaps sixteen standard years—cleared his throat and said, "You stand before Her Excellency, the Lady Gadar Berhane Amtarra-Vaha Malyan

VII, Baroness of Thagura, Archon of Pseldona Prefecture, and Lady of the Rock."

I swept my gaze over the cup bearer. He was bare chested, and wore only a white cloth bound about his waist. Unable to keep a faint frown from my lips, I went to one knee. Taking the offered hand, I knelt and kissed the Baroness's signet ring. "Lady Malyan, I've come to give you back your world."

Gadar Malyan withdrew her glittering appendage. She smelled of salt, and I guessed that she had been swimming in anticipation of our arrival. Standing, I drew back to a level with Valka and Pallino.

The Baroness smiled lazily, staring up at me. "Hadrian Marlowe. I expected you would be taller!" Her tongue curled catlike as she grinned. "It is an honor to meet you! We are gratified to learn the Emperor has sent his best *at last!*"

"The honor is mine, my lady," I said, and fixed my eyes—as was the military custom—on a point over the lady's shoulder. "The Emperor will be relieved to know that you survived."

"Certainly he will be," she said, her grin freezing on that marble sculpture of a face, eyes gone hard as glass. "That, no doubt, is why he has left us to languish under the alien boot for so long. *The sun is high, and the Emperor is far away,* they say. But I thought Thagura counted for more in the Imperial books than this."

I frowned at her. It was an old Mandari proverb she quoted me, from an age when that people had emperors of their own, but she used it wrongly.

"I beg my lady's pardon," I said, and bowed my head, letting my confusion go. "We came as swiftly as we were able, and set out not two days after your message came. We were at Monmara when we received our orders from the Solar Throne. It was a long journey."

"The Throne itself?" She brightened. "The Emperor himself ordered you to come?"

"Yes, my lady," I said, eyes flickering to her face and away. A bead of water—or was it sweat?—was tracing its line down her white neck, and where it ran I glanced dutifully away from. The order had, in truth, come from the Imperial Council, from the war minister, Lord Bourbon, and from the director of Legion Intelligence. But it was best let her believe as she liked. If believing the order had come direct from Caesar softened her disposition, that was just as well. "I have orders to bring you to Marinus to meet with Lord Hauptmann and the Viceroy. They wish a full report of what has transpired here."

Gadar Malyan's perfect lips twisted, but settled on a smile. "I will be able to tell my tale in person? To plead for my people?" She almost rose from the divan. "Are we to go now?"

"Not at once," I said. "The Cielcin have been driven from orbit, but it may not yet be perfectly safe to move you. I wanted to ensure that you *were* safe and to put my men at your disposal. I have brought half a hundred of my men to help keep you safe until we are certain the system is secure."

"Only half a hundred?" She almost pouted. "So few?"

"We detected no Cielcin ships within a hundred miles of your city," I said in answer. "There may be a knot or two on the surface, but nothing that should give us much trouble. Even now my people are preparing to land in force and secure what remains of your city."

"And what of yourself?" she asked. "Are you staying?"

Hooking my thumbs through my belt, I answered her. "I would hear what happened."

"Yes, yes you must!" she said, her lazy smile returning. "Send your servants away, my lord. We haven't much, but we shall make you as comfortable as we may. Will you not sit? Ravi! The wine!" She waved one bangled arm at a chair beside her divan.

I moved to accept her invitation, swept my cloak aside, but seeing there was no other chair near at hand for Valka, I asked if one might be brought.

Malyan's face turned downward. "Are you not going to dismiss your servants?"

"I'm not his servant," Valka snapped, angling her chin.

Eager to head off any incident, I raised my hands. "Lady Malyan, may I introduce Valka Onderra Vhad Edda. My companion."

"Your companion?" Malyan's eyes flickered from Valka's face to mine. "Your concubine?"

"His paramour," Valka corrected, using the very word I'd avoided with Captain Maro. I caught myself blinking at Valka in surprise. She had spent much of the years since Vorgossos in cryonic fugue, and though I had aged five years since she first kissed me aboard the ship of Kharn Sagara, she had scarcely counted one, and so her admission surprised me, so cautious had she been to give our entanglements a name before.

"Paramour, really?" Gadar Malyan reclined against the rest of the divan, breasts heaving beneath the gauzy shadow she wore as she accepted a goblet from her serving boy. Speaking round the rim of the glass, she inquired, "There's a wife, then? I had not heard."

Why were we talking about *me*? I looked from Valka to the Baroness, back to Valka as she replied, finding her tongue before I could: "I am all."

"I'm sure you are, dear," Malyan said, black eyes taking Valka in. "I'm sure you are."

Before Valka could conjure a reply, the boy Ravi approached with a chair from further down the way and set it beside my own, so that Valka and I faced the lady as she reclined, raising her goblet for the boy to charge. He did so dutifully, and it was only as he did so that I marked the hollow quality and glassiness beneath the charcoal that rimmed his eyes. Like everyone in the vaults beneath the Malyans' Rock—everyone except the Baroness, it seemed—the boy was exhausted body and spirit. When he had finished with his mistress's cup, he poured for Valka and me before drawing back, his shoulders hunched.

"He is such a good boy," the Baroness said wistfully, gazing at her servant. "The last of his house, I daresay. His father, Lord Vyasa, was my archon down in Aramsa."

Turning to look at the boy, I found his eyes were on me, hard as glass. "I am sorry," I said, and to the Baroness, too, I added, "We'd have come sooner if we could."

"I know," she said, and lifted the goblet to her lips. "But it *is* over, yes?"

"Yes," I agreed, and tasted the wine. It was Kandarene, and red as arterial blood. No wine of Earth was ever so bright and violent a color, nor so thick. "Will you tell us what happened?"

QUEEN AMID ASHES

The Baroness set her goblet aside. "What is there to tell?" she said, adjusting the drape of her garment. "They overwhelmed us. They were in orbit before our deep system satellites flagged them. My captains told me the surveillance grid was ill-maintained."

"Your man Maro said as much," Valka said, eliciting a terse expression on the lady's face.

"Did he?" Malyan asked, chewing her tongue. "Maro is very good. Very thorough." She drummed her fingers against the bowl of her goblet. "But my fleet never stood a chance. The Cielcin outnumbered us five to one, I'm told—ship-for-ship—and their flagship! You can scarce imagine! There are moons about our outer planets that were smaller. We were fortunate Thagura does not have much by way of seas! We might have drowned, you know?"

Lady Gadar Malyan shifted where she sat, leaned forward to place her glass on the table between us in such a way that her shift fell open. She caught my eye in the fraction of second my attention slipped, and smiled. Her own eyes flitted to Valka as she covered herself and sat up. "They besieged Pseldona that same day. Dropped . . . half a hundred landing towers on my city. Mother Earth alone knows how many of my people they made off with. My men were overmatched."

"Is that when they burned the city?" I asked.

"Oh no! That . . ." she caught herself. "*They* burned it later. Their prince—Muzugara, I think his name was—sent a herald to order my surrender. I refused, of course. I can't imagine my capture would have done much to dissuade his men from sacking my world."

My fingers tightened on the goblet they held. *Our swords*

shall play the orator for us.

When I had gone into the tunnels beneath Emesh to first confront our enemy, I had done so in the hope that I might reconcile our two kinds. As a boy on Delos, I had dreamed of traveling the stars, of seeing man's dominion, and of meeting the xenobites that dwelt beyond and beneath us. Not just the Cielcin, but the Irchtani, the Cavaraad, the Umandh, and all the rest. I imagined that the war that plagued mankind and the Cielcin both was all a misunderstanding, that surely we could be made to coexist. That it was only human greed and human cruelty that kept us apart.

I was half right.

We are no angels, we men. But the Cielcin?

Too well I remembered the screams as Aranata and its men tore our captured crewmates limb from limb and feasted. When I closed my eyes to blot out Gadar Malyan's failed and obvious attempt at seduction, I saw instead white, inhuman faces raised to watch me, red and smeared with gore.

Five years since Vorgossos. Five years and the nightmares had never quite stopped.

Aranata's blade flashed at my neck.

Darkness.

"You're quite right," I told the lady. "There is no reasoning with them."

When I opened my eyes, I found the Baroness watching me with one eyebrow arched. "My fleet was lost. Every ship in orbit—nigh on every ship I had—was destroyed within the first month. Archon Vyasa and the lesser lords launched what resistance they could. Perhaps the exsul houses on the edge of the system came to our assistance, I don't rightly know."

QUEEN AMID ASHES

"Perhaps they fled," Valka said.

The Baroness dismissed this with a gesture, neither denying or allowing this. "We lost our satellites after the first sack of the city. Muzugara's ships used them for target practice. For a time we communicated via the old hardlines, but those were lost before the first year was out. We had the telegraph, only none of the in-system numbers answered. Not Vyasa, not Acre, not the exsuls. What could we do but wait?"

"Waiting seems to have suited you quite well." Valka's tongue cut the air like a razor, like highmatter.

I flashed a glare at her, but she didn't seem to notice. Her eyes were on the Baroness, who leaned back in surprise. "Perhaps you should consider a wife, my lord," she said to me, ignoring Valka as one might a barking dog. I felt my own blood boil. "Your woman speaks above her station."

If Gadar Malyan expected me to apologize for Valka, she was fated for disappointment. "She's Tavrosi," I said, an explanation—not an excuse.

"She is most uncouth," Malyan said. "Though perhaps such wild blood has its benefits."

"That is quite enough, Baroness," I said. The woman was palatine, and of higher rank than I, but I was a knight of the Royal Victorian Order, one of the Emperor's own, and her liberator. "So the Cielcin firebombed the city?"

Malyan blinked, fetched her goblet, for a moment uncomprehending. "I . . . yes. In the second year. They took out the bastille sooner, and the palace of course. A few other targets, but they spent their time harvesting the population. I gave orders to evacuate to the countryside as soon as they arrived, but I don't know what good it did."

"To the countryside?" I echoed. "To the desert, you mean?"

Malyan shrugged. "That is what countryside we have on Thagura."

I clenched my jaw. Too many of the great lords of the Empire I have known have thought too little for the men and women in their charge. Only Caesar himself ever seemed to care. Him and perhaps a few precious others. I never understood them, these men and women—like my own father—who viewed mankind not as man, as men and women, but as ants, as numbers on a balance sheet.

Pallino spared me the trouble of responding, for he hurried back up the steps wither he'd departed, boots pinging off the hard walls of stone and echoing about the bare forms of the caryatids. "Had!" he exclaimed, forgetting formal protocol in his haste. "We got word from Corvo! They've pacified high orbit. She's sending troops down to secure the city as planned, but there've detected Cielcin dug in near the pole! Corvo says there's camps up there. Miles and miles of camps!"

"Prisoner of war camps?" Valka asked, rising to her feet.

I felt my blood run cold despite the heat and the damp beside the pool. I had seen holographs taken at Cielcin war camps before, but only still images. The longhouses—tents, really—and the ill, starved people crowded into pens. The bodies and human refuse piling about the ankles of the living. Pestilence, famine, and death. I did not want to go, but knew I must.

My chiliarch nodded behind his faceless mask. "Most like. She's launched an attack group to take the camps. They'll be there in three hours."

"Can we join them?" I asked, rising as well. "Is there time?"

"I thought you were staying!" the Baroness objected. "Am I not to go with you?"

It was the boy who once had dreamed of peace that moved me. If my men took Cielcin prisoners, I might speak with them. If I could speak with them, I might find a way to peace, might repeat what I had done on Emesh—might use our prisoners to barter with Muzugara, *somehow*. If I could turn even *one* of their clans to our cause, it would be progress and *proof* that things could change, that the Crusade that had for four centuries racked the galaxy might end at last.

Drawing my cloak about my shoulders, I said, "Plans have changed, my lady. The enemy is still on your world. Pseldona may be safe, but I would not risk your safety. You must stay here until the security of your planet can be guaranteed." To the room at large I said, "I will leave my guard with you, my lady. For your protection. Valka, Pallino." I gestured, and without waiting to be dismissed, hurried to the steps.

"You're not thinking of leaving *me* here, are you?" Pallino asked when we had returned to the hall. Maro had remained behind a moment in the wake of my sudden departure, no doubt consoling his lady for the rudeness of her rescuer.

Fearing we might be overheard, I took Pallino by the arm and leaned in. "There's something amiss here, Pallino. The Baroness is far too cavalier for a woman who lost her entire world."

"Ten years ago," Pallino said. "And being trapped down

here so long's enough to drive anyone a bit mad."

"She was trying to seduce you," Valka said, appearing between us. "You saw how she reacted to *me*."

"Is she that desperate?" I could hear the wry grin in Pallino's voice, and flashed him a look. It was not the time.

I could only shake my head. "Possibly she thinks her family is done for. With Thagura ruined, maybe she thinks throwing herself at me will save her. I don't know. She could just be putting on a brave face, but circumstances have been so dire here for so long. . . . I want you and the men to hold here and keep order. There's bound to be a bit of unrest now these people know the end has come."

"I don't like it, Had, sending you alone." Pallino placed an arm on my shoulder.

"I'll take the shuttle and link up with Corvo's attack group. Did her message say who had the command? Crim?"

"Aye."

CHAPTER 3

THE SATANIC MILL

FIRES WERE ALREADY burning by the time our shuttle landed on the ice beyond the perimeter of the sprawling camps. So far to the north, not half a hundred miles from the frozen pole, the sun would not rise for years—so long were Thagura's seasons. The angry red glare of the fires chewed at the ranks of broken Cielcin landing towers like malformed trees, and the light of that burning set the snow and ice to gleaming like rivers of molten glass. In the distance, a fusillade cracked and rolled like thunder, and as we entered our final approach, I saw the shapes of our men hurrying to and fro between the various grounded ships that formed our little command post.

I had already donned my helmet, and so could not smell the smoke of the great burning as the shuttle ramp lowered and I hurried out, flanked by the two guards I'd allowed Pallino to send with Valka and me when we left Pseldona. The unseen energy-curtain of my shield muffled sound, as well, heightening my sense of dislocation. Nonetheless, the roar of engines overhead and the blast of distant guns drummed loudly in my skull and chest. How could I have thought it like thunder?

It shamed the thunder.

The command frigate lay just ahead, parked on the snow like some lost beetle beneath shields of its own. A small fleet of our troop landers nestled about it, their ramps down, holds empty, the snow about them trampled or melted where our legions had passed. Through the smoke and swirling flakes, I could make out the shapes of the rear guard dug in behind sandbags and snowdrifts about the landing zone, their gleaming artillery at the ready, waiting for the Cielcin counterattack that might never come.

"By damn, 'tis cold!" Valka swore. "We couldn't have docked with the frigate direct?" She alone of the four of us was not armored, and the cloak she'd taken from the shuttle was hardly enough to keep out the cold.

"Not landed, ma'am," said Oro, the senior of the two guards and the man who'd served as herald on our arrival. "She's a *Roc*, that one. The holds are all along the ventral hull."

"It isn't far!" I said, wrapping an arm and my own cloak about her.

The four of us hurried across the snow. I had to resist the temptation to duck as lightercraft winged overhead. It would not have done for the men to see the Halfmortal crouching like some back-bench logothete afraid of fire, but the noise of the fliers was a holy terror, and it took an effort to keep upright. As we drew near the *Roc*, a trio of men hurried forward from an auxiliary ramp to greet us. Two were legionnaires in red and white, their faces hid. The other was a lieutenant in the blacks of a naval officer, one of the new men the Emperor had assigned me when he'd elevated me to the station of knighthood. She wore a white, fur-lined cloak over her greatcoat and held her matching red beret to her head to keep it from being blown off by the wind.

"It's Bressia, isn't it?" I said, relying on my suit's amplification to boost my voice over the wind so I did not have to shout.

"Yes, my lord!" the lieutenant replied. "Lieutenant Commander Garone asked me to bring you to him! This way!"

No sooner had the words escaped her lips than a flash of violet light split the polar night like a wedge, and overhead a line of our Sparrowhawk fliers tore toward the camp. One of the Cielcin siege towers—standing like the rockets of uttermost antiquity—had been preparing to launch. The roaring we had all been shouting over was not mere gunfire, but the distant fury of ignition as its great engines blazed. The light of red fires painted the bellies of the clouds as the black tower rose sluggishly toward heaven, but it was too late. The Sparrowhawks' beam weapon had found their mark, and for an instant I stood transfixed upon the snows as that dark tower fell back to ground in a nimbus of golden fire.

The Cielcin would not escape Thagura. Not alive.

Lieutenant Bressia escorted us up the ramp and through the hold to the bridge of the grounded frigate, whence Lieutenant Commander Karim Garone directed the assault. Like most of my high officers, Crim had been a mercenary before he cast his lot in with me and my Red Company, one of the Normans who had served Emil Bordelon on Pharos. Being Norman and of Jaddian descent, he had spurned the blacks and silvers of the Imperial navy uniform, dressed instead in the braided dolman and kaftan that were his custom. Even aboard the bridge of the *Roc,* he wore his shield-belt with its white ceramic saber and the well-worn bandoleer that glittered with knives.

He was one of the deadliest fighters I'd ever known, and more than once I'd guessed he had been an assassin for some Mandari oligarch before I found him, for he was an easy killer and as cunning as a fox when it came to fighting.

"Glad you made it, boss," he said, straightening from his examination of the tactical display. "We've crippled what little fleet they had. Bombed the landing field on our way in. Lighters are taking out what we missed."

I returned the commander's lazy salute, ignored the momentary stiffness and quietude of the lesser officers in the command post. Most of them had never so much as seen me before. Thagura was our first mission under the Imperial banner, and while the senior staff was composed primarily of *my* people, the Normans who had fought for me at Vorgossos, the bulk of our new officers' corps and nearly all our enlisted men were Imperial levies, men and women assigned to my service by the Emperor when he gifted me the *Tamerlane.* Almost I could feel their eyes crawling over me, examining every line of my face and of the black cloak and sculpted cuirass that had likewise been a gift from the Emperor.

"I didn't miss it!" I said, thinking of the thunder and fire we had witnessed outside. "I saw your work! You're sure none have escaped to orbit?"

Crim smiled. "Small good that would do them! Even if one of them slipped our nets, those landing towers of theirs aren't warp-capable. They could get to orbit, but then they'd have nowhere to go . . . and Corvo and Glass and the fleet to deal with."

"Very good," I said, joining him by the display. Still I could feel eyes crawling over me, and glanced round at the junior men seated at their duty stations in the stark light. One or two looked hastily away, and all returned attention to their work.

Somewhere to my left, a hushed voice whispered, "Halfmortal . . ."

I flashed a glare in the direction of the voice, but could not find the speaker. Peering down at the topographic projection on the tactical display, I asked, "What of the enemy?"

"They're dug in, that's for bloody sure," Crim said. "Been up here a long time . . . but the place isn't heavily fortified. Looks like they weren't expecting any trouble up here."

"We're a thousand miles from the nearest settlement; I'm sure," I said. The Cielcin were subterranean by nature, unused to the light of stars. Lost in years of sunless night, Thagura's north polar region made for the ideal place for them to establish a beachhead, with so much of the planet's lower latitudes given over to desert and savanna and sun.

"Petros took his chiliad around to the east," Crim said, and pointed, highlighting where the Cielcin had erected a palisade of overlapping plates. Guard towers—more landed rockets, I deemed—stood at intervals along the wall. "Sword Flight's hammering the towers."

"When did you engage?" Valka asked, coming to my side.

Crim answered, "Three minutes past two, ship time." I checked my wrist-terminal. That was nearly half an hour before. We'd arrived sooner than I thought.

"Gravitometers are showing huge pits bored into the ice beneath several of the buildings." The commander gestured at a number of red-highlighted cylinders thrust deep into the glacier.

I heard Valka's frown in her voice. "Geothermal sinks?"

"Maybe?" Crim replied. "If they are, they're not lighting up like they should on thermal imaging. Might be shielded."

"Or something else entirely," I said darkly, glancing from the projection to the thin stripe of window that ran along the forward wall of the bridge. Smoke rose in a mighty wave from the burning camp, and the firelight flooded through that horizontal slash of a window like blood from an open wound. "Are there captives?"

Crim followed my gaze. "Survivors, do you mean? I'm not sure. That's why Sword Flight's sticking to the towers. Dascalu and Ulpio took their chiliads straight forward, toward the south wall. Here." Again he pointed, highlighting the alien palisade directly between the landed fleet and the camp proper. "They're to keep the Pale from breaking through and taking a run at us. Petros is there—on the east as I said. One of the groups will get through. If there's anyone still alive, we'll find them." He met my eye, and his face hardened until it seemed as stony as Aram's colossus. "How was the city?"

"Gone," I said. "The Pale blasted it from orbit. Atomics, maybe. Plasma. I'm not sure."

QUEEN AMID ASHES

"*Noyn jitat.*" Crim exhaled. "Earth rot their bones."

Valka gripped the rail of the console podium. "Perhaps there are survivors."

"We can hope!" Crim said, and wheeled round to stride up the central aisle toward the window and the spot where the helmsman's and navigator's stations stood, one hand on the hilt of his sword. "M. Irber! What of those towers?"

A dark-haired ensign at one of the tactical displays raised his voice in reply, "Just need a little more pressure and time, sir. There are seven on the eastern perimeter still firing. Sword Flight's swinging round."

Drumming his fingers against the hilt of his sword, Crim said, "Righteous."

"Fifth Chiliad's pinned down on the ice, though," Irber continued. "Towers 12 and 13 have clear lines of fire on their approach."

"Raise First Sword," Crim said, turning to join Irber by his console. "Order his wing to concentrate fire on those towers. I want Petros to have a clear line against those walls."

Valka leaned toward me and asked, "First Sword?"

"The aquilarii," I said, meaning the fliers. When we were but mercenaries in the Norman Expanse, we had had no air force of our own, no lighters. Though Valka had been a ship's captain in her youth, that had been for the Tavros Orbital Guard, and their ways were not our own. "Their wing leader."

While Irber relayed his orders to the wing commander, I brushed past the holograph podium and stalked toward the window. Another flash of violet light cracked the sky and bled its color on all creation.

My first *real* battle.

But not my first brush with violence. That had come in the streets of Meidua when I was young. Nor was it my first encounter with Death. The old crone had visited my father's house when I was just a boy, had taken my grandmother from me. For just an instant, my eyes—reflected in the smoky alumglass—seemed *her* eyes, preserved forever in the blue fluid of the canopic jar I'd carried down the steps to our necropolis in her funeral train. And I had known war, had ventured beneath the surface of Emesh and into the bowels of Vorgossos . . . and into the Howling Dark that awaits us all. But Emesh and Vorgossos had been small battles. Desperate battles, aye, and fierce, but small.

Thagura was something *else*.

But I was a knight then, and at forty *finally* a man, though by rights my ephebeia ought to have happened half my life before. Before I had led of necessity, led because I alone possessed the *pothos*, the *vision*: my *dream* of peace. But that was—quite literally—another life. That dream had died with Aranata's prisoners of war, and with me. On Thagura and after, I led because I needed to. I led because I had a duty, and a purpose, and a mystery to solve.

Understanding why the Quiet had restored my life required that I serve the Emperor, for I knew the Emperor possessed knowledge of that ancient race, and that he alone might command his magi to illuminate me.

And I fought because it was right—or so I told myself, consoling myself while the screams of Aranata's prisoners echoed in the black vaults of my mind.

"Are you all right?"

Valka had come up beside me, was peering up into my face with her luminous yellow eyes. How strange it was—even then—to see softness on a face so long hardened and sharp as glass. We had not begun our acquaintance well. She had thought me simple, a barbarian, and despised me for it, as she had despised the Empire I called home. After so many years of coldness and disdain, seeing concern on her hard but lovely face was like returning for the first time to a place in spring that one has only ever known in winter.

"I'm fine," I said, responding in her own tongue so we might not be overheard. "I've never really commanded an army before."

"'Tis not so!" she said, smoothing the cloak over my shoulders. "You led the charge from the *Schiavona*. You saved all those people."

I took her cold hand in my gloved one. "That was different."

"'Twas not."

"I didn't have a choice, then. I didn't have time to think about it."

One corner of her mouth lifted in wry bemusement. "And now you have the time for thinking you are not so sure?"

A short laugh escaped me, and I looked round to see what eyes were on us. There were none. The helmsman's station and the navigator's were both empty with the ship grounded as it was. Another flash of violet cut the night, and the distant thunder boiled as the earth shook. Irber shouted, "That's Tower 12!"

When I did not reply, Valka turned me fully to face her and leaned against the console. "These people's lives are in my hands, Valka," I said. "This *planet* is in my hands."

"'Tis what you wanted, is it not?" she arched an eyebrow. "A purpose?"

What man is a man who wants less?

Or more.

She glared up at me, eyes truly glass, bright as crystal. Reaching out, I took her hand. "I wanted peace."

"And if you can't have it?"

I found I could no longer look her in the eye. I could not say what I was thinking. The words would not gel. Perhaps I had no words at all then. I have them now. There will always be peace. It is only a question of when. War is energy, and energy runs down. The universe returns to rest, and whether that rest comes without any conflict or *after* it is another matter entirely.

"We will have peace," I said, and stooped to kiss her. She did not shy away.

I did not say, *One way or another.*

※

Smoke rose from the field like a swarm of locusts, like a shoal of black fish writhing in turbulent waters before the coming diver. Crim and Valka had both objected when I announced my intentions to join our chiliads fighting in the camp—Crim because he felt his Commandant should not risk his life in what was still an active war zone, and Valka because I had ordered her to stay behind.

"We have no armor for you!" I told her, though armor might perhaps have been found aboard the frigate. It was a lie, and she knew it—but I did not dare to risk her, though

QUEEN AMID ASHES

I gladly risked myself. Men are ever more careful with the lives of their loved ones than they are with their own. Still, I understood her fury. Valka had been a soldier once—after the fashion of her people. She had been a ship's captain long ago, had even known battle—if once and briefly. But she was no fighter, and but for our ill-fated adventure on Vorgossos, she had never known personal combat, had never fought an enemy sword-to-sword, or fired her old service repeater in anger. She had no experience leading men or fighting tooth and claw with the enemies of man.

Ahead, the watchtowers that ringed the inhuman camp guttered like dying torches. To our left—where the snow drifts piled high against the palisade—one had fallen entirely, and the blue lightning of ruined circuitry spat in the frozen air.

Our shadows danced tall and shapeless on the red snow before us as we hurried forward, cast by the great lamps on the landing craft at our backs. Crim had ordered thirty hoplites for my escort, shielded men armored red and white. Not far ahead of us, a full century—mixed light and heavy infantry—hurried toward the shattered gate that opened on the alien base. The violet crash of hydrogen plasma and silent flash of beam weapons lit the polar night as the air ahead resounded with the cacophonous music of human and inhuman voices. The men about me might have been living statues, faceless and mechanically precise in their movements, communicating over direct bands or by brisk signs. Above our heads, the knife shapes of Sparrowhawk fliers circled slowly by, floodlights shaming the light of the burning towers. The whole of the air thrummed from the oscillations of their repulsor drives until it seemed the whole world lay beneath the skin of some almighty drum.

I might have been alone in all that movement—the only true person on Thagura—were it not for the screaming, for the occasional noise on the comm line.

"Up ahead! On the right!"

"—get a clear line on the target!"

"Form up, men! Form up!"

"—think the bastards fired some of their own ships!"

"You seeing this?"

"The walls! Earth and Emperor! The walls!"

This last came from one of the men of my guard. We'd come to just within a stone's throw of the palisade by then, the tips of our shadows just tickling the foot of the iron wall. The alien structure had been erected without any intention of permanence, though it might have stood for years. It was fashioned of great interlinked sheaves of metal shaped like leaves—like the scales of some unholy terror twenty feet in height—and each was crowned with a row of spikes perhaps a cubit high.

Atop each spike a misshapen gourd hung skewered, some perched at the very tip, others thrust to the base so that the iron rods ran *through* them. Snow half-covered them all, but I knew at once what they must be, realized it with horror in the instant before one of the men nearest me cried out.

"They're heads!" came the shout from just behind me.

"Mother deliver us," came another voice.

I had seen men beheaded before. Hanged. Whipped. Thrown in stocks before the halls of justice on a dozen Imperial worlds, even in my home in Meidua. I have seen the bodies of prisoners hanging in gibbets for the sport of crows, seen branded criminals begging for coins, carrying their bowls in their teeth for want of hands.

I know that men are not angels.

But the faces yawning down at us from the wall had been *savaged*. Cheeks flapped in the wind, faces torn open ear-to-ear. Eyes were missing or else hung by slender cords. Scalps were torn and bloody or torn away entire, and every face bore the mark of tooth and talon.

The will that raised that wall and set that camp in order was cousin to our own. It had taken an intelligence not unlike the intelligence of men to build that fortress and the rockets that encircled it. An intelligence . . . and an understanding of physical law. But the spirit that had done such violence was the spirit of an animal, and though man was beast himself and capable of terrible violence, that place was like nothing I had dared dream.

It was the dryness of it that so shocked me. That was the thing.

The armies of men had, of old, piled heads as high and done things as cruel, but always to some purpose—or so it seems to me. To frighten an enemy or break him, to encourage obedience or discourage revolt . . .

But the blood upon the wall was frozen and dry.

They had not done this thing to frighten *us*. These were old dead, wind-bitten and frosted over. The Cielcin had intended no statement by their actions, meant to issue no warning. They had done all this for themselves, and only for themselves.

This black thought hounded me as we reached the level of

the ruined gate and passed beneath the watchless gaze of that broken humanity. One of the Sparrowhawks slewed overhead, drifting on its repulsors, its gunner picking targets from the camp ahead with admirable precision.

"Dead ahead!" cried the decurion on point before me. "Fire! Fire!"

I saw what he had seen an instant later. One of the longhouses stood dead ahead, and indeed five of them converged on a yard just within the gate like the spokes of a wheel. The doors of the foremost longhouse stood open, and lit by the fires that blazed within, a dozen warriors stood tall and thin and terrible as Death herself. Taller than any man they were, but narrower in the shoulder and longer of limb, like shadows stretched by the light of dying sun. In the red light of war, their slick, gray armor might have been green, but their pale faces—white as chalk, as bone—shone terribly even at this distance. Even as we drew near, one among them leaped toward our men who'd gone before and lay into them with its scimitar tall as a man. The milk blade flashed, crashed through the shields of two hoplites—left, right—for there is no shield that man has made sensitive enough to turn back the meager energies of a sword blow.

Two men fell dying, and the beast that slew them fell an instant later as a dozen plasma rounds struck its face and chest. My own chest tightened as the memories of war came flooding back, but I clamped down on my fast-galloping heart, clenched my unkindled blade in my fist, and rushed forward to battle.

Where that first warrior fell, two more leaped into place, each wielding not the milky blades of their kind, but whips like braided cords of silver, which they uncoiled and—whirling above their heads—let fly.

"Snakes!" cried one of the men about me in warning.

The silver whips writhed through the air between our party and theirs fast as any arrow, rolling on repulsors. I squeezed the twin triggers of my blade and raised the weapon in reflexive guard as they slithered in among us, swimming through the air chest-high. The blade shone blue-white as distant stars amidst the angry reds of all that burning, and the exotic material rippled as the liquid metal blade shaped and reshaped itself with every motion.

"Hadrian!" Valka's voice sounded in my ear from where I'd left her on the *Roc*'s bridge. "Hadrian, what's happening?"

"*Nahute!*" I said, drawing my blade high. They were machines, the weapon of a Cielcin berserker, flying snakes whose steel and diamond maws clamped, lamprey-like, to their prey and drilled into them, seeking the heat of a man's body and center mass. How many men have I seen chewed and hollowed out by such weapons? How many thousand?

Our shields would buy us time, and indeed I saw the first drone strike straight for one hoplite's face and rebound as his energy-curtain repelled the shot, but they would snake among us, would worm their way in slowly, through the shield, and do their lethal harm. Fast as they were and slim, they were tricky targets for any man with lance or plasma burner, and they were then among us.

My men were too close. I could not strike at the drones without carving through them, and nothing—save adamant and highmatter itself—could stop that highmatter blade. One man screamed as one of the *nahute* pierced his shield and found a gap in his armor. Red blood smoked in the freezing air as his suit's integrity failed.

"Spread out!" I shouted, waving my sword above my head. "Spread out and fire on the Cielcin! Fire on the Cielcin!"

The men all moved to obey me, and the xenobites pouring from the longhouse ahead began falling, but not before many threw *nahute* of their own. The drones flashed among us, and leaping aside I struck one in half with my blade while above, the torch-beam of one of the Sparrowhawks passed overhead, so that the snow of the yard—trampled gray by so much traffic—shone hard-edged in every detail. Shots rained down from above as the belly-gunner picked his targets.

Beside me, another man fell screaming, wrestling with one of the serpent-drones as it bored into his side. I ran to him, seized the tail of the horror as it wriggled in deeper. The dying man looked up at me, and from the angle of his blank visor I knew he was staring straight into my eyes. Though I pulled, I knew I could not get the snake free, and the poor bastard went limp an instant later.

When he was gone, the drone slid out easily, but before its spiral maw could turn to strike at me, I slashed it clean in half.

The skirmish had ended without my notice. The bodies of men and xenobites littered the yard or else lay piled by the doors of the burning longhouse. Shaking the blood from my hydrophobic cape, I straightened beside the body of the dead man and—blade still burning cold in my fist—stumped to that open portal.

Safe in my suit, I had no fear for air, and on account of the fires there was sufficient light to see what lay within.

QUEEN AMID ASHES

The bodies to which I guessed the heads belonged hung skinned and bound by their ankles, their blood left to drain through a kind of grate laid upon the floor. There must have been hundreds of them in that longhouse alone, each hanging like some hideous fruit. Many had their arms missing, and so little resembled men or women at all, but those that did hung down from on high, trailing like a forest of kelp from the floor of some grasping sea.

I turned away as quickly as I could, and was glad of my mask and helmet to hide the sickness and horror in my face. Still sensing that something was amiss with me, one of my decurions came and put a hand on my shoulder. Voice amplified by the speakers in his suit, he asked, "My lord? Are you all right?"

I wanted to vomit, but found the words instead. "This isn't a camp," I said, choking. I had known intellectually, had known all my life, that the Cielcin devoured the flesh of men, had seen the frenzy fall on Aranata's prisoners aboard the *Demiurge*. But to see so many lives ended, so many human persons treated with such systematic industry . . . it was a horror unlike anything I had faced, more terrible even than the Brethren who dwelt beneath the waters of Vorgossos. "This isn't a camp," I said again, more strongly. "It's a slaughterhouse."

CHAPTER 4

DEATH BY WATER

AS MUCH AS MY heart cried out to let the fires burn and make a holocaust of that unholy place, prudence and wisdom both demanded I order them put out. An examination would need to be made of the camp. Holographs and phototypes needed taking, and reports needed making. Despite four hundred years of war, there was much—too much—of the enemy that we did not then understand. Though I speak their tongue and though I'd set out on my quest to understand them and to make peace, there was much—and more—I did not myself then understand.

And much I could not believe.

The camp seemed unreal to me, a nightmare uplifted through the bedrock of sleep to disturb the waking world. It was a horror unlike anything I dared dream. Such horrors there are in human history, but they are only shadows. Imitations in our halting human way of the deeper horrors and depredations of the Pale. Of the Pale and of the black gods they serve. The Cielcin have no compassion. I know that now, though I then hoped it might prove otherwise. If they extend mercy, it is because they require something still of those shown mercy. If they surrender, it is ever with the thought of revenge, or else because their spirit has broken utterly. Often I have wondered if they may truly be called evil, for a tiger—as I have said—is only hungry when it hunts and slaughters man.

When such doubts stir in me, I return to that camp.

The heads on the walls had been placed facing *inward*, peering down at the survivors laboring in that living hell. The lips of many had been cut away, or torn by inhuman fangs, so that they smiled on the men and women below. When I remember it, my doubts boil away within like mist before the sun.

Evil *is*.

The tiger is not cruel, nor the tidal wave. The meteor is blind and the solar flare heedless as it burns. Men are cruel—and beasts sometimes, yes—but they are men. And the Cielcin are Cielcin. What peace is there to brook between predator and prey?

"My lord?" inquired a rough voice over the comms. I recognized the voice of Dascalu, one of my new chiliarchs. An instant later his name and ident code flickered in one corner of my suit's entoptics.

I was standing in the middle of the yard just inside the ruined gate, snow and smoke roiling all about me. Above, a trio of our *Ibis* shuttles circled, repulsors gleaming blue against the polar dark. Fire retardant fell like rain from nozzles in their underside, and slowly the conflagration began to ebb.

"My lord?" Dascalu's voice intruded again. "My lord, you should see this!"

Shaken from some dissociated reverie, I at first mistook Dascalu for one of the men around me, and said in reply. "No one should see this."

There were still intermittent sounds of fighting in the middle distance as our troops encountered a new knot of the enemy barricaded in some outbuilding or in the tunnels we were just starting to find beneath the ice. A staccato burst of gunfire sounded just then, as if to punctuate my reply.

"What's that, my lord?" asked the decurion next to me.

Realizing my mistake, I shook my head, keyed the comm response. "What is it, chiliarch?"

Dascalu's response came after the barest hesistation. "We're in the southmost of those domes along the western wall of the complex. We've found…well, I don't know what we've found. Some kind of monument?"

"Monument?" I echoed the word. "What do you mean?"

"That's what it looks like. Petros said I should call it in."

An image appeared in one corner of my display. I studied it a long moment, stomach turning over, my cloak pulled by the snowy air. "I'll be right there," I said at last. "Forward your images to Dr. Onderra at the command post." Turning to the men of my guard, I gestured that they should follow and began crossing the yard. The men had piled the bodies of the enemy in a great mound in the center of the yard formed by the five slaughterhouses, and the few dozen of our dead had been laid in neat rows along one side. Moving toward the domes—which were visible just over the flat roofs of the longhouses—I switched comm channels, broadcasting to all battle groups. "What news of survivors?"

"Negative, my lord," came Petros's reply.

"Nothing yet," said Dascalu.

"No sign," replied Ulpio.

We passed between two of the slaughterhouses and turned right, following a path of compacted snow past what I guessed was the intake for the longhouse in question. My mind sketched the images of men and women in rags herded barefoot and bloody through the shutters then closed.

"Holy Mother Earth, have you ever seen such an awful place?" one of the men at my back muttered, voice flattened by his suit.

I could only shake my head. Had I known such places existed in creation, I would never have taken Uvanari alive at Emesh. I would never have left Delos at all. I felt sick, and longed for a bottle and the sweet oblivion of sleep.

The camp was not large, covered perhaps a dozen hectares, perhaps two. The palisade with its row of ruined heads encircled the thing entirely, buttressed by the then-blasted or fallen shapes of the siege towers. The gate by which we'd entered—the gate nearest the slaughterhouses—had been nearest the broader landing field, whence more of the alien landing craft now smoldered, the first casualty of our assault. Later reports would funnel in of similar camps, all of them clustered in the north polar region where the sun then little shone, for the Cielcin were creatures of the underworld, reared in caverns beneath the skin of their homeworld, and their eyes little loved the light.

Beyond the far end of the longhouses, a series of squat towers marched. These were the lower segments of siege rockets, I realized, pods dropped by the xenobites to serve as housing units for the xenobites themselves, for the slaves and slave-soldiers of Prince Muzugara, whose job it was to tend the prisoners and administer the camp.

"Why couldn't they build somewhere warmer?" one of the men muttered, trying not to be overheard by me. "Thagura's half desert, ain't it?"

"Cold's got to be hell on the prisoners," another man agreed.

"They aren't prisoners," I said. "They're food. Did you not see the bodies?"

The men went deadly quiet behind me. My brother Crispin's voice resounded in my ears, his old question, asked at table so long ago. *Is it true the Cielcin are cannibals?*

Cannibals they were, and worse. Anthropophagi.

"Enough talk," I said, voice dark and flat through my suit speakers. I turned to face the men, who—deadly quiet—went deathly still. "This is not a camp. Do you understand? It is a *ranch,* one meant to dress provisions for the Cielcin fleet. When I said it is a slaughterhouse, I meant it is an *abattoir.* The Thaguran population was brought here, *processed,* and shipped to the Cielcin fleet. That is why they have been here for these ten years." I shook my head. "We will not find many survivors. Hundreds, perhaps thousands on all this world."

The men made no reply, but shifted awkwardly where they stood. One ducked his head.

I turned away.

Half a dozen domes, each some five hundred feet in diameter, stood along the western wall of the camp complex. Snow covered each of them, but here and there that shroud lay cracked, broken by the ridges in the dark material beneath it. I felt certain that these were built of the same interleaving plates as the outer palisade, a light and quick construction designed to provide rapid protection from the snow and wind. Thagura was warmer than Earth of old had been, but still the ceaseless winters of that frozen north froze deep enough to kill a man in hours.

More inhuman bodies littered the approach to the low slit of an entrance, and more of our men stood armed and vigilant along the path. The snow there was trampled black by so much foot traffic, and a broad, shallow sort of gully ran down to the rim of the dome, where a sort of tunnel led beneath the dome itself and inside.

What doors there might have been were gone, blasted to shrapnel by the breaching charges my men had used to get inside. Picking my way over the tangled limbs that clogged the descent, I passed under the shadow of the arch. The walls to either side were carved from the polar ice and studded with bits of alien electronica whose functions I could only guess at. Ribbed cables ran along the walls and across the floor. The tunnel turned sharply right, following the curvature of the dome overhead. The few lights that yet functioned were red and dim as dying suns, and my suit's entoptics boosted the image projected on my eyes to compensate, contrast sharpening until the hall seemed a simulacrum of itself, unreal.

Seeing how cramped the confines were, I turned to my men.

"Decurion, you and your men with me. The others will wait here and guard the entrance." I did not wait for his reply, but hurried along the passage ahead.

Catching sight of me in my black mask and armor, one of the legionnaires in the hall thumped his compatriot, and the two stood straighter. A third hurried forward. "Lord Marlowe, the chiliarch sent me to retrieve you."

"Where is he?" I asked.

"Just inside," the man said, saluting a little late. "This way."

Turning, he led us past more stationed men and over more bodies, following the icy corridor along its gentle curve. The hall slanted steadily down, deeper into the ice, and I felt certain the air must be bitter cold. Half a dozen men waited at an inner door below and stepped aside at my approach.

The image I had seen briefly on my mask's display greeted me at the bottom of the stairs. We had come out beneath the black metal of the dome, and from beneath, its structure revealed itself like the petals of some venomous flower, black and razor-edged. The apex must have been two hundred feet above our heads, and all about us the native ice rose twice the height of a man to where the spiked foundation posts of the dome rested in the planet's surface.

The Cielcin had melted a space for themselves beneath the dome and I spied a number of side passages that led to further tunnels, doubtless connecting to the other domes that lined the western edge of the camp. About the walls were stacked barrels wrought of some gray cousin of plastic, and heavy crates marked with alien runes. Dead ahead, in the center of the room, a steep-sided pit—like a well—opened in the icy floor. Great chains, hung from cranes bracketed to the dome above, descended into the shaft. I might have wondered at their purpose had I not been distracted by the horror erected along the wall opposite.

"Holy Mother Earth, deliver us," I, who did not pray, hissed.

Skulls lined the wall opposite, set in a broad arc that must have circled a full third of the circumference of that chamber beneath the dome. Each was polished clean of flesh and shone in the low light. Inhuman hands had set them there, and stacked them high and neatly, rank upon rank, their hollow eyes staring down at me, asking, *accusing*.

What took you so long?

Each had been nailed to the ice wall of the chamber, pinned through the back of the cranium from below. The sculpture—for sculpture it surely was—rose two dozen heads high in the center, where a central column, undulating, rose from the ranks massed about the base. These rose like a wave of skulls above the tide, like a serpent standing, ready to strike.

For the second time that day, I thought I might wretch, and shut fast my eyes against the sheer *number* of them. There must have been thousands.

"My lord!" A familiar voice startled me from my horror, and opening my eyes I found the chiliarch, Dascalu, hurrying toward me. "We called as soon as we were sure the dome was secure." He gestured at the wall of bones. "What is it?"

I shook my head, not daring to speak for the gorge rising from churning stomach to burning throat.

I had never seen anything like it before—not on Emesh, not on Vorgossos. Ice crunched under my feet as I circled the pit toward the effigy. Beneath my mask, my mouth hung open. I felt increasingly sure that I was looking at some crude impression of a snake. The Cielcin had placed each skull with care, with reverence, with malefic intent. Curling tendrils snaked from the central column like arms, coiled across the surface of the ice, each wrought from femurs and tibias and the long bones of countless arms.

For what felt then the hundredth time that day, I thought I might be sick.

"I don't know," I said at last, when Dascalu asked again.

I was reeling, drowning in ignorance. I had thought I knew the enemy, thought I'd learned my lesson aboard the *Demiurge*. A knight I might have been, and cloaked in Imperial favor, but I was *so* young, and for all my reputation, I was a fool as all children are fools. Forty years actual might have made a man, if only technically. But it is experience that makes men in truth, and though I had felt myself a man when I drank the Baroness's wine, I felt a child in the shadow of that fetish to the Pale's black and deathless god.

I would see such sculptures many times, on many worlds.

They never got easier to see.

"They piled what looks like spoils from the people here," the chiliarch said, gesturing to a pile of rags and various oddments high as a man that lay mounded between the arms of the macabre display. "But that isn't all." He pointed—as I knew he must—at the pit. Dascalu shook his head. "My lord, I . . ."

I raised a hand to quiet him. I didn't need to hear.

Black water waited at the bottom of the pit, its surface disturbed by the movement of something unseen within it.

The Cielcin had melted a shaft down into the glacier—it must have been twenty feet to the dark surface.

"Is there a light?" I asked.

"Torch!" Dasculu shouted, casting about.

One of the men at hand produced a glowsphere about the size of a grapefruit and passed it to the chiliarch, who handed it with deference to me. Without comment, I pulled the tab. The thing vibrated and flared in my hand, and a cold, white light, fierce and several times brighter than the alien lamps, filled the domed chamber. Not engaging the lamp's repulsor, I let it fall. The light vanished down the shaft, hit the surface with a distant *splash*.

The waters churned as things pale and eel-like swam away from the light. The glowsphere sank like a fallen star, illuminating the waters.

Those waters were not black at all, but *red*.

"Those things aren't native, are they?" Dascalu asked.

"I'm not sure," I told him, studying the monsters. Each was about as long as a man's arm, and milk-white. "Valka?"

Her voice sounded in my ear, "I'll look."

But I didn't need her answer. I knew. They were Cielcin creatures, some species of fish-like organism brought from the circle of some dark star.

"What are they for?" the chiliarch asked.

The glowsphere had reached the bottom of the shaft then, had settled on the bottom. Its white light had colored pink from the waters below. How deep those waters were was hard to say. It might have been half a hundred feet. That redness was clue enough, but I knew what I would find at the bottom, and sure enough, there they were.

QUEEN AMID ASHES

More bones lay mounded at the base of that shaft, stripped as clean as the ones mounted to the wall.

I drew back, overtook by a vision of men and women crowded into this place and forced into the waters a dozen at a time. Had they been living when their Cielcin captors fed them to their worms? Or were these the cast-offs? The men and women not fit for the slaughterhouses or for a life in chains aboard Muzugara's ships?

"We'll need to get a science team in here," I said. "Radio Captain Corvo and the rest as soon as you're sure the compound is secure. Ask for Varro and his best."

I heard Dascalu salute, but did not turn to look at him.

"Would that we'd come sooner," I said to no one in particular.

"'Twas no way we could have done," Valka said into my ear. "We came as swiftly as we were able."

I bit my lip. "I know," I said, and wrapped my fingers around one of the frosted chains that ran down into the horrid pit.

Dascalu had not left my side, and I found him peering down with me. Presently he ventured a question. "How many do you think there are down there?"

"We have no idea how deep it goes," I said, eyes moving back to the serpentine icon wrought of human bones. "And all these must have been down there once." A terrible thought occurred to me, and I asked. "Is it the same with the other domes?"

Dascalu's silence confirmed my deepest fears.

"But why?" I asked, shaking my head. "Have you ever heard of anything like this?"

"No, my lord," the man replied, glad to have a less weighty question to answer.

I thought I knew them. The thought kept rebounding in my head. *I thought I knew them.* Since I had been a boy, learning their inhuman tongue at Tor Gibson's knee, I had dreamed of traveling among the xenobites, among the pale Cielcin who wander the stars in ships like homeless moons. I had read everything in our limited collection there was to read on their culture, their biology. What little we men knew, we knew from war. From the hulks that littered our star systems or broke upon our shores when their raids had come and gone. Though our two kinds had warred for centuries, there was much—so much—we had yet to learn. But for a few symbols, their written language was still a mystery, and though we knew their weapons and their warships, understood their tactics, much of their culture, their literature, their art, remained obscure. I might have been one of our Empire's foremost authorities on the enemy, but I knew too little.

We all did, in those days.

"Look out!" A shout shocked me back into my body, and turning I saw a hulking, black shape leap into the central chamber from a side passage, its white sword flashing in the misty air. Two men fell before it, weapons discharging, punching holes in the surrounding ice. One shot grazed a conduit, and power sparked and died, plunging all the low, red lamps the xenobites had fixed to the walls into stygian black. Only the distant shine of the glowsphere at the bottom of the pit lit the chamber, and by its glow I saw another trio of Cielcin cut their way into the room. One tackled an armored centurion to the ground, pinning his arms like an aggressive lover as it lowered its fangy jaws to tear out the man's throat.

Conscious of the pit at my back, I darted to one side, circling right to hit the intruders from the side. I ignored Valka's questions ringing in my ears and snapped my sword from its magnetic hasp. Dascalu had moved to follow me, and the few of my guard who had stayed with me scrambled to adjust their bearings.

One of the Cielcin hurled its *nahute* toward us, and my men fired at it before the chiliarch roared. "Bayonets! Bayonets, hold your fire!" That stray shot had, after all, destroyed the dome's lights. A second *nahute* flew at us, and its owner chased after it, sword drawn to strike at the men before me. My guardsman raised his energy-lance to parry the alien scimitar, and he twisted, struck the monster with the butt of that lance.

The Cielcin staggered against the wall, huge black eyes glaring. With its sword, it battered the man's lance aside and slashed at his neck even as the *nahute* drone impacted the man's shield, disorienting him. The soldier fell like a toppled tower, head striking the ice wall. Not realizing he was already fallen, the *nahute* found a chink in his armor and burrowed its way in.

The xenobite's eyes found mine, and blade dripping it advanced on me. "*Tuka yukajjimn!*" it barked in its rough tongue. "*Tuka eja-ayan!*"

You are vermin! It said. *You are nothing!*

"Nothing?" I echoed, repeating the word. "*Eja-ayan?* You have lost! Surrender!"

In answer, the tall xenobite bounded toward me, raising its sword. I raised my own, fingers squeezing the triggers to kindle the liquid metal blade. The highmatter fountained from the hilt, pentaquark nuclei locking into place. The Cielcin blade descended, met mine without resistance. The alien blade sheared clean in half, and the part that should have struck my head clattered against my shoulder. For an instant, the xenobite stood clutching its stump of a sword, black eyes confused. I guessed it had never seen highmatter before, did not know that it was already dead.

My own blade rose and fell, bit into the monster's shoulder and slid clean through from collarbone to the opposite hip. The creature fell in two pieces, and I stepped into the space it had occupied a moment before, bloodless weapon gleaming in my fist. The two behind it stumbled back, adjusting to this new development. One launched its *nahute* at me, while the other uncoiled its drone and cracked it like the whip it so resembled.

Reflex made me draw back, recoiling even as Dascalu and the hoplite at my side moved forward, lances aimed at the small knot of survivors who had burst into the room. I held the right flank by the wall, with Dascalu at my left and more of the men hemming them in. There was shouting and a tight burst of plasma fire—despite the chiliarch's orders—as the men at my left slew the *nahute* the enemy had let fly.

"Where did they come from?" the decurion asked.

"I don't know!" Dascalu answered. "We swept the dome! I swear it!"

Our men had encircled the remaining Cielcin then. They had nowhere to go but back along the side passage whence they'd come. Thus cornered, trapped on Thagura, their ships burned, their fleet fled to the outer Dark, they had nothing but to give up their lives.

"No matter!" I shouted.

There were seven of them left. Seven against the sons of man. Seven against Earth.

The fighting stilled then, if only for a moment as either side measured the other. The Cielcin were all taller than us, slim and crowned with horn. The tallest among them—an officer of some kind—must have been eight feet high. The lesser berserkers wore versions of the gray-green armor the warriors above had worn, the livery of Prince Muzugara. If the cold bothered them, they gave no sign, each crouching, adjusting their posture, daring us to attack.

The fighting would be over in instants if we could be sure of our aim, but I understood Dascalu's caution. We outnumbered the Pale at least three-to-one in the chamber, and more men were not far. We had only to summon reinforcements.

"Take them alive if you can!" I said, surprising the men about me.

"Sir?"

"You heard me!" I said, then barked a word to the xenobites. *"Svassaa!"*

Surrender!

"Surrender?" the officer echoed. "There is no surrender! Not to vermin like you!"

"You will die here!" I replied, wary of the discomfort the inhuman words coming from my lips placed in the hearts of the men about me, but I had studied their tongue since

I was a boy, and though no man may speak it properly, I spoke it as well then as any man could.

The officer held its *nahute* limp in one hand. "We are dead already! Our prince is gone!"

"He abandoned you!" I agreed, adjusting my guard. "But surrender and I will permit you to die honorably. You may take your own lives, so that you did not die at the hands of us *yukajjimn*."

The thought seemed to tempt the xenobite for a moment. The officer hesitated, hands slackening on its weapons. Its round, black eyes searched for some evidence of my eyes in the black sculpted mask that hid them. It did not find them. "Those are not our orders."

"Damn your orders!" I said, and said again, *"Svassaa!"*

The officer flinched—a curiously human motion. "We are Cielcin," it said. "Cielcin obey."

"Your prince does not!" I replied. "He commands! And he is gone."

Still the officer hesitated, and only then did I mark the wound on one temple above the narrow hole that served it for an ear. Ichor dark as ink ran down the far side of its face. Sensing that I had knocked it back a step, I continued, "You have the command of these." I gestured with my sword at the others. "Are you not now their prince? Do you not now command?"

"Dunyasu!" one of the others roared. "The worm speaks blasphemy! Mutiny against our master!"

"I have a shot!" interjected one of Dascalu's lancers.

"Dunyasu!" another of the lesser warriors agreed. "Don't listen to it, Emasu! It lies like all its kind!"

QUEEN AMID ASHES

"I have a shot!" the lancer shouted again.

The underlings chose for us. The two who had cried out *dunyasu*—abomination—leaped forward like gargoyles from the buttresses of a chantry. I jumped aside as one bowled into Dascalu, knocking the chiliarch from his feet. The violet flash of an energy beam felled one of the others, and in the next instant I saw the officer, Emasu, fall as invisible light scorched its shoulder.

I cursed, and ran my sword through a swung *nahute* as one of the warriors whirled the serpent-drone over its head. Another cut stole the legs from under the demon, and it fell, blood smoking where it met the ice. My own bootheels crunched, and I slipped as a third stroke took the head from the downed creature. My knee struck the ground, and I groaned as Valka hissed a sympathetic word in my ear.

The fighting was done before I stood once more, reduced to a blurring of slow movement on the ground as the dying died. Dascalu had emerged victorious, clutched a bloody knife in his off hand as he staggered back to his feet.

"Give that to me!" I ordered him, and the chiliarch did not argue. I snatched the bodkin from him, held it reversed, with the blade flat under my arm.

Unkindling my sword, I went to the wounded officer, and seizing it by its horn forced it to look into my masked face.

"You are dying," I said flatly, voice amplified by my suit. "You may yet die well. Answer me: What is this place? What is it for?"

Emasu blinked up at me, nictitating membranes flicking vertically across its eyes. Confusion? Surprise? "*Paqami wo,*" it said. *We must eat.*

The thought of men hanging skinned and headless in neat rows flared brightly in my chest, and, straightening, I released the demon's horn and pressed the heel of my boot against its wounded shoulder. Emasu winced, and before it could move I pointed the emitter end of my unkindled blade in its face. "The pit!" I said, leaning my weight onto my foot. "The statue! Explain!"

Emasu's eyes went to the sculpture of bones, the many-armed serpent rising along the interior of the dome, almost to the metal leaves that formed the roof over our heads. "*Miudanar!*" it said. "The Dreamer!"

Miudanar.

It was the first time I ever heard that hateful name. I knew it not then, but I looked for the first time upon the likeness of one older than Time. Miudanar the Great, the Dreamer, who dead and deathless sleeps until the stars burn down.

"Miudanar?" I asked, stomping upon Emasu's shoulder. "Your god?" I had never seen any of the Cielcin gods rendered in art before. Had never seen any art from them save the round glyphs—like clusters of bubbles—that passed for calligraphy among their kind.

In answer, the officer groaned. "His is the time before time, and the time after it."

Emasu hissed as my heel dug into its wound. "You killed my people to make an idol?"

"*Veih!*" the officer said. "No! These were the scraps. The leavings, and those who could not work, or would not serve to nurse our young."

Behind my mask, I blinked. "Your young?" But I shook my head. It didn't matter. I held Dascalu's knife up for the officer to see. My meaning clear, I pressed, "Are there survivors? More of my kind?"

Emasu eyed the blade with emotions I could not name. Longing, perhaps? Disgust? Relief? "We could not kill you all. Below ground. There are pens." It jerked its head back the way it had come, down the side passage that had been sealed before the assault. "We waste nothing. Even your kind has its purpose!"

I pressed harder, and the officer cried out in pain. I didn't care. The hollow eyes of so many thousands glared down at me—I hoped—in gratitude and belated triumph to see the predator so vanquished. "You wasted plenty when you torched the city. How many millions died that day?"

"We didn't burn the city! That was you!" Emasu tried to sit up, and snarling I stomped it back into its place, making the men about me fumble anxiously with their lances. "We would have sucked it dry if we could. Taken our fill and fled! But our fleet was starving! We could not leave without our fill, and your kind breeds but slowly! We could not replace what you took from us that day!"

Emasu's words rattled me to the bone, and I *did* stagger back then, reeling as I turned my back. "They didn't burn the city," I said numbly, speaking so the other men would understand. The full horror of what it was saying—that they had forced the human captives to breed more food, that they required us to help *nurse* their young—was lost for me in that moment beneath the weight of this *other* revelation. Speaking in Cielcin once more, I shouted down at Emasu. "What do you mean you didn't burn the city?" I was almost screaming.

"It was you!" Emasu hissed. "Your kind! Your ships!"

I staggered back, taking my foot from the inhuman officer's shoulder.

"They didn't burn the city," I said again. "They didn't . . ." *Malyan did.*

I thought of the devastation we'd seen in Pseldona, the ruins of the city stretching for miles across the shelf above the desert, blackened, sand burned to glass. If what the monster said was true, it was not the xenobites who had wrought that devastation, but the very woman whose duty and sacred charge it had been to defend that city with her life.

"My lord, look out!" Dascalu exclaimed, raising his lance to fire.

Whirling, I found Emasu half-risen to its feet, claws extending from its six-fingered hands like so many knives, teeth bared and black with blood. It never found its footing. Before it could stand, a dozen men discharged energy beams into its body, sending up faint coils of white smoke in the dim air. Dead, the officer teetered a moment and fell back where it had lain a moment before. Disgusted, I raised Dascalu's knife and hurled it into the body. To my surprise, the blade stuck in the xenobite's throat.

A sudden need for air overcame me, and I clawed at my helmet. The casque broke apart and folded away into the neck flange of my armor, and tugging at the elastic coif that bound my hair I sank to my knees before the pit, gasping at the frigid, stinking air. It was worse—far worse—than the sterile closeness of helmet had been. When Dascalu approached and put a hand on my shoulder to check if I was all right, I seized it and glared into his visored face. "It

QUEEN AMID ASHES

said there were survivors down below," I said. "Find them, and bring them to the ships."

"Yes, my lord." Dascalu turned to go.

I did not release his arm. "Dascalu."

"Yes, my lord?"

"Do not let the survivors see . . . any of this."

"Yes, my lord."

CHAPTER 5

THE SURVIVORS

"I WISH YOU'D have let me go with you," Valka said.

We were alone for the moment in the command frigate's ready room, a spartan chamber in the usual Imperial gloss-black, brass accents worked into the walls and about the imitation window that showed the smoldering ruins of the camp. I could just make out the domes, snow-frosted, in the distance, black against the blacker sky.

Seated in the high-backed chair at the head of the ellipsoidal table, I glanced at her. "I know. But you weren't kitted for it. It's cold out there."

"'There would have been time for me to find a suit if you'd but waited," she countered, her eyes flashing. "'Twas no need for you to rush into the heat of things."

"It wouldn't have been right for me to sit here safe on the ship while the men seized the fortress," I said in reply.

Valka held my gaze a moment, silence stony.

"I have a duty to my men," I said, spreading my hands defensively.

"You have a duty to *lead* your men," she riposted. "Do your knights not lead from ships such as this?"

Her golden eyes had started boring holes in my face, and I turned to look back at the ember-lit camp through the false window. "I am not those men," I said. "I don't have the head for strategy. That's for Crim. And it isn't right that they should risk their lives while I stay safe on the bridge."

The smile in Valka's voice shone through. "Hadrian, you really were born ten thousand years too late."

"Twenty thousand," I countered, taking her point.

Before she could respond, the door opened, and the chiliarchs, Dascalu and Petros, entered the chamber. Both men had removed their helmets, and their red-and-ivory armor still bore the grime and damage of battle. Both saluted in unison, raising gauntleted hands, but it was Petros who spoke, looking by far the worse for wear. An ugly bruise colored the left side of his face, doubtless a relic of the fighting. "My lord, we've brought our wounded and the survivors most in need of care to the ships, but it'll be another ten hours before the *Tamerlane* is in position to drop shuttles enough to carry the survivors out of here."

"Ten hours," I chewed the figure like something sour. "How many are there?"

"More than ten thousand for certain, possibly so many as fifteen."

"Fifteen . . ." I rubbed my eyes. It was a staggering figure, perhaps more than we could transport south in a single journey, perhaps more than we could adequately provision and care for if Thagura was truly as devastated as it seemed to be. But to be all that remained—if they were all that remained—of forty million? "So few . . ." My tongue felt swollen in my mouth. "Do we have the provisions we need to bring them south?" Pseldona was gone completely, but there was a chance that one of the lesser cities had enough infrastructure in place to help sustain so many.

Petros shook his head. "That's a question for the captain. We can bring them south, but all the bromos protein on the *Tamerlane* won't feed so many for more than year or two. They'll have to get to planting or starve."

Half-turning to Valka, whose perfect memory would ensure the task did not go undone, I said, "We'll need to telegraph Nessus. Tell them to send a seed ship. These poor people won't survive without offworld aid." The sick feeling that had not left me since the doors of the slaughterhouse opened only intensified. There would be more death on Thagura in the years to come as the survivors worked to decide just what life after the invasion would mean. "And I'll want the aquilarii to scout the countryside. All wings. I want the message broadcast to every corner of the planet: Thagura is retaken. Let the survivors come to every city and be counted. I want to know where any and all survivors might be. If there's so much as a fishing village intact that can take refugees, they must."

Petros nodded, turned his dark gaze on his associate. "We think we found the people you were looking for. Survivors from the city. Took a measure of doing. Once it got out we were looking for those who survived the sack, all manner of folk lined up."

"But you think you found any people who were really there?" I asked, knowing that many would be only desperate fools looking for any opportunity for bread and care.

"Not many, and they aren't well," Dascalu put in. "Pseldona was rocked in the first weeks of the invasion. The poor bastards have been in the camps all this time. Pale used them for workers."

A shadow passed over Petros's face at the words, and I had to remind myself that the chiliarch's own home had been devastated by a Cielcin horde. He knew what it was like to live under alien occupation, to see people taken and used, to see others turn against their fellow man for an extra few months of life. "Collaborators, most like," he said. "Take what they say with caution, my lord."

I held the chiliarch's eye for a solitary moment. It was a trick I'd learned from my father. Say nothing, let the other man chastise himself. Prudent as his advice was, he should not have offered it without my asking.

Realizing his error, Petros looked down. "We can bring them to you at your convenience."

"Please," I said. "Send them in."

There were nineteen. Nineteen men who had survived the ten years since Pseldona burned. Most of the other survivors had come not from the primary cities—from Aramsa, Tagur, Port Reach, and the rest—but from the lesser cities and townships that dotted the planet in the wetter, temperate zones above the ergs that dominated the equatorial regions.

They were all men, not a woman among them. My men had forced them to scrub in the sonic showers aboard the command ship, and each had been given a standard issue single-suit of unmarked black to wear. Many were missing ears or fingers from so long in the polar night, and though nearly all were darker skinned from generations in the deserts that girdled the world, there was a sallowness in their complexion that spoke to years without light. Thagura's seasons were long, its orbit slow, and so in all the years the Cielcin had spent sucking the blood and life from the planet, the long nights and short days so far north had not even begun to reverse.

They shuffled through the door, each emaciated and skull-faced, pale eyes bulging at the sight of Valka and myself and at the faceless men of my guard. Several sat at the table without being ordered to do so, and I did not reprimand them for it. These men had lived in hell, and needed no more of it from me. I could then scarce imagine the horrors they had known, and that failure of imagination held my tongue for several long instants while the poor men waited for me to speak.

I do not have to imagine now, for I have lived as they lived, and for nearly as long.

Had I then known, I would have spoken sooner, for the sound of any kind word would have been like drops of rain in a desert. "Gentlemen," I said after another long moment passed, "I am sorry."

No one spoke, and how could they? What were my words measured against the breadth of their suffering? Had I the panacea of the ancient alchemists to hand, it would not have served them. The marks of talon and lash—and those of teeth—could be seen upon their hands and faces, but I sensed the deeper wounds lay in their souls. There was a hollowness in every face, a cadaverous light in every eye, a light that illuminated *nothing.*

My words were nothing.

And yet I knew I must speak, and so opened my mouth. "My men tell me you come from Pseldona. Is that so?"

A couple nods, but mostly vacant stares greeted me.

"I am sorry," I said again, and found my own eyes sliding to the polished black glass of the table between us. "That is a very long time."

"My family!" one of the men burst out, dark eyes meeting mine. "My lord, do you know them? Lorna and Emin? Are they alive?"

There was a desperate hope in his eyes, one I'd no choice but to snuff out. "No, no, I don't know."

The man crumpled into his seat, and the instant he did so every other man began in the same vein, shouting one over the other for news of his family, his children, his parents, his wife or lover. They shouted until the hard walls rang with the rough sorrow of their voices. I felt the tears rise in me, and shut my eyes to stem their flow.

I raised a hand, and only steadily did quiet fall back into place. Confusion, hope, despair . . . all hung upon the air like incense. "We only just freed the camp," I said. "It will take time to learn who all we have. My men tell me there are thousands. It may be that some of your people have survived, but I don't know. I don't know yet."

The new silence deepened, and almost I could see the dark cloud settling on every heart. But I had to know, had to ask, and so proceeded. "There is something I want to know, something I was hoping you all might be able to confirm for me." Not a one of them would meet my eye, their hopes all crushed or forwarded as they dreamed of hurrying through the other survivors themselves, scrambling for any sign or symbol of those they'd lost. "During our attack on the camp, I interrogated one of the enemy. An officer, I think it was."

"You spoke to them?" one of the men asked, shaken from his torpor. His pale eyes shimmered as he looked at me, horror plain in his face. "With those demons?"

Valka placed a hand on my shoulder, quiet support. The man sketched the sign of the sun disc before extending his first and final fingers in the ancient warding gesture against evil. Others did the same. I was well used to my familiarity with the xenobites' tongue frightening people, nobiles and plebes alike, but in that room it was something different. The mere admission that I *could* treat with the enemy placed their stamp on me, as surely as the Emperor had placed his stamp upon me with his ancient sword. I was tainted, attainted, *touched* by evil. To the poor captives, it must have seemed that they had not escaped at all, but had fallen from the hands of the enemy into the hands of one who was half-Cielcin himself.

But I would not lie to them, for lying has never ordered the world, or made it better. "I did," I said, and felt the temperature drop about me. "And it told me something I think only you gentlemen can confirm. It told me that they were not behind the bombing of Pseldona. It told me that *our* forces—the Lady Malyan's forces, that is—were the ones who destroyed the city."

I could still hardly get the words out. The mere thought

was more sickening than the camp itself. Why would Gadar Malyan do such a thing? I thought back to my meeting with the Baroness, and to the Lady herself, nearly naked and dripping from her swim. She had planned to seduce me, that much was clear. Had she hoped to distract me? To play the ingenue, to place the blame on Vahan Maro or on some other officer—now dead? Or was she really that simple? Really the vapid and sensual debutante she'd presented? I couldn't be sure, but there was a sour taste in my mouth, edging more bitter with each instant I reflected on our meeting.

"It ain't true!" said an earless man by the door. "Her ladyship would never do such a thing. She's ruled us since my grand da's day, and her family's kept Thagura since the beginning! Four thousand years! She'd not do such a thing! Not never!"

"Aye!" said another man, his left eye and the whole side of his face wound in fresh bandages. "The lady would never. Seen her, I have! Like Mother Earth herself. It was her engineers what brought the water down from the north and saved my village."

"Your village?" Valka interjected. "Are you not from the city?"

The man stammered, looked down, as if shamed by her question or caught in some lie. He flushed, "That was when I was a lad, 'fore I come to Pseldona."

We were all quiet then. For my part, I could not quite tell if the man was lying or no, but I supposed it didn't really matter. Surely one of the nineteen was from the city itself. I would not punish the men for lying. In retrospect, I should not have offered a boon to anyone with information. I knew that generosity was like to bring forth liars, and I should not have been surprised to find one or two had slipped by Petros and Dascalu's net.

The vehemence with which these men defended their lord surprised me, though. My father had never encouraged such loyalty from his people, but then my father had been a different sort of ruler, inspiring fear, not love.

Hadrian, name for me the Eight Forms of Obedience. Gibson's words floated back to me.

Obedience out of love for the person of the hierarch, I thought, imagining these peasants seeing the statuesque Malyan from afar. Genetically perfected by the magi of the High College, she was a goddess to them. How could they not love her?

I ran a hand back over my hair, pushing the dark fall from my face. How long had it been since the medtechs had taken me out of fugue? I glanced at my wrist-terminal. Not quite three days. Ye gods, I was tired. Had I slept at all? I thought I must have dozed on the flight from Pseldona to the pole, but I could not remember it. There would be too little sleep in the days ahead. I would need what I could get on the flight back to the city.

"There weren't no raid sirens," a voice interjected.

Looking up, I could not at once identify which of the men had spoken, but after a second or two those around him gave way, carving out an empty space between them and the speaker. Thinking back to Petros, to his contempt for these survivors, I wondered if just that behavior had been a part of how these men had survived for so long, and felt a shred of my chiliarch's contempt.

The man who had spoken was old, though perhaps it was only his torment which so aged him. The tip of his nose was gone, and one ear, and claw marks marred the side of his neck.

"I'm sorry?" I said.

"There weren't no raid sirens, *my lord,*" he said, taking my question for anger at his failure to use the proper honorific. A felt a pang of guilt. "Remember it plain as, I do. I worked down in the greenhouses. Out on the edge of the erg. Lord Aram—the first Baron, I mean—he had raid sirens built all through the city. All up in the rocks, like, so as folks would know to shelter if Extras or some other house come raiding in from the Dark."

"It sounded!" another man interjected.

"When the attack first came," the old man said, "aye. And the second time. When the Pale come and raid the city proper, by Blue Square and all. But they didn't sound that next day."

The man who'd interjected, a flat-nosed fellow bald as an egg, interjected again, "You've gone and lost it, man!"

"I have not, Lodi! It's you who don't remember!" The old man looked around at me. "I'd not lie to a nobile, my lord. Not for anything. On my honor!" Obviously nervous, he scratched at the ruin of his nose.

Eager to head off any interruptions from the man called Lodi, I asked. "What's your name, sir?"

"Siva, my lord. If it please you." If the man had had a hat he might have wrung it in his hands.

"Tell us what you were going to say," Valka said, and something softened in the freedmen, as though it were a relief in itself to hear a woman's voice. I wondered again that there were no women among them.

The man Siva let his hand fall from his frostbitten nose. "We were sheltering, sheltering in place as ordered. There weren't no proper bunkers down on the sands, but there was the old biostation out by Sharkey's Point. That's where we were when the bombs dropped. Lucian—he were in the Legions once—said they weren't no atomics, but I don't know the difference. Bright as twenty suns they was. Blinded a couple of us, and I still don't see right out my left. Didn't stand a chance when *they* came circling back. Figured it was *them* what done it, but there was no sirens, I'd swear by Earth's bones, my lord, begging your pardon."

"I think he's right," said a younger man from the back. Scarred as he was, the man's accent betrayed a greater polish than that of the others. "I was in the city. In one of the public shelters. I don't remember sirens that day. And they didn't come for us until later. The Pale, I mean. Months later. We had to open the vault when the water went bad. That's when they found us."

I glanced up at Valka.

"They said the sensor grid was decimated in the first attack," she said, speaking Panthai so as not to be understood.

I nodded, remembering, and replied in kind, "It doesn't take a satellite grid to know a fleet's incoming. Warning might have come later, but not at all?"

Our use of the Tavrosi language seemed to perplex all but the man with the urbane accent, and I returned my attention to them. "There is a very real possibility that your lady ordered the bombing of Pseldona," I said, as measured as

I could manage. To my surprise, the men did not burst out in objections this time. "What her motivations might have been, I cannot say. Perhaps she had bad intelligence in her bunker. Perhaps she thought the enemy had taken the city. I don't know . . ." I tapped one of the magnetic hasps that held my white Imperial cloak in place over my armor. "I am a servant of the Emperor, and no other man. If she has done this thing, I must know of it. His Radiance must know of it. And I will find out."

"Shouldn't you be worried about *them?*" asked a man from the rear, hard-eyed and obviously half-blind. "Not pointing fingers at her ladyship?"

"She brought water to our village!" the man who was *not* from the city blurted out again. "When I was a lad. Folks were dying they were, and she saved us!"

A third man cried out, "The Pale are still out there!"

His words set the other men to shouting: "They took my Ari, they did! Killed her in front of me. Put her head on the wall!"

"And my Lorna! And my boy, my poor boy . . ."

"It's them you ought to deal with!"

Eyes shut again, I forced the words out sharp as I could make them, though my voice shook. "The Cielcin have been driven from your system. Their fleet is gone."

The man called Lodi shook his head. "They'll be back, then. The minute you're gone, they'll be back. They'll not leave so easily. They know we're here."

Unable to keep quiet any longer, Valka exclaimed. "The Cielcin have done all the harm they can to Thagura. They'll move on to some fresh target. 'Twas only desperation that kept them here. They were underprovisioned for another journey."

"It may be they'll have to eat one another before they reach wherever they're going," I said, thinking back to my conversation with Emasu and with Aranata Otiolo—before it killed me. That prince's people were starving too, suffering from so long a time in space, with so little food, so little protection from the radiation that bathed the Dark between the stars. I had pitied the Cielcin at the time, but my capacity to pity them had worn through, like old shoes I'd walked too many miles in.

My words seemed to perversely comfort the men. Looking around, I said, "The Cielcin will not return here. Not in your lifetimes . . ." Nineteen pairs of eyes—mostly pairs—looked back at me with bruised hope. "You will all be taken south as soon as possible. We are scouting for a place to move you and the other survivors. Somewhere warm! My men will see to it that each of you receives a wine ration before you return to your tents. Tell the others their suffering is at an end." I waved a hand to indicate they were dismissed.

The men shifted where they stood. Some turned, others rose unsteadily from their chairs.

One coughed, and the younger man with the scars and the city accent asked, "What is your name, my lord?"

I glanced up at Valka, hesitating in the knowledge that these men would return to the refugee tents we'd ordered erected on the ice. They would share the news of this meeting with the others as they shared or hoarded the wine rations we gave them—each according to his nature. It felt strange to take credit for their freedom. I had not won the battle in orbit, though I had briefly confronted Muzugara over the holograph. That victory belonged to Otavia Corvo, to Bastien Durand and the other ship's officers. I had been only an accessory, a part of the audience. Nor had I smashed the camp and freed the prisoners, though I had done my best to stand in the thick of it alongside my men. That victory belonged to Crim, to Dascalu, Petros, and Ulpio and the other chiliarchs, to the wing commander of the aquilarii.

Valka spoke first, addressing the men. "This is Lord Hadrian Marlowe."

Looking back, that moment stands out to me, not because it was the first such moment, though in a sense it was—the men whom I'd saved at Vorgossos were my own, and knew me—but because it was in another sense the last. There was no recognition of that name in the faces of the men, no opening of eyes and mouth, no reverent whisper of *the Halfmortal*. I was only a man to them, as I had not been to my own people aboard the *Demiurge*. I would not be a man much longer.

I had just become a name, and names are seeds whence heroes grow.

The city man bowed deeply. "Lord Marlowe. I am called Antin. Thank you. I . . . thank you."

Several of the others bowed, or bowed their heads.

"Thank you, Antin," I said awkwardly, and felt Valka's hand once more upon my shoulder. The old man who had first spoken of the raid sirens had reached the door, and I said, "M. Siva, would you please stay?"

The old greenhouse laborer froze. Head bobbing, he turned back, frostbitten hands over his heart. "Yes, lordship."

QUEEN AMID ASHES

Antin was the last to go. He lingered on the threshold a moment, looked back at me one last time, and I knew that he would be the one to take his tale to the others, the thousands who waited in the tents. His story—not mine—would be told to the survivors of Thagura and spread like a virus. In a generation, there would be songs and tales of how Hadrian Marlowe alone stole into the camp and freed uncounted thousands. How with his own hands he tore the gates asunder and stormed in while his men set fire to the alien ships. I might have smiled if the thought were not so discomforting.

I did not want to be a hero. That was not my dream.

"M. Siva," I said when the door hissed shut at last. "I'm sorry to keep you, but I must know. Were you holding anything back for fear of the others?"

The old man shook his head, but did not raise his eyes.

"M. Siva, I must know." Still the old man did not speak. "I will not bribe you," I said, "but if you know something, *I* must know it." Valka moved and seated herself at my right hand, placed a hand on the table near to the old fellow, comforting as best she could. "Was it the Baroness's forces that bombed the city?"

Siva screwed shut his eyes, and I realized in the next instant that he was shaking. Valka reached out and took his wrist. "'Tis all right," she said. "No one will know you told us."

The laborer bit his lip, shook his head furiously, but he said, "It wasn't *them*." He sucked in a deep, rattling breath. "There were no warning. No sirens. No bells. It were the third day. *The third day*—didn't even give us a week to fight back. I'd gone out with the basket to raid the greenhouses—

they hadn't smashed them yet, hadn't bothered with the outskirts. The others as could had taken all the skiffs, the groundcars . . . emptied the bloody motor pool. We was trapped. Couldn't run if we wanted to, and anyway, Pseldona was home. I thought it was them when I first see 'em flying in. They came out of the sky, down from orbit. But the Pale landed those towers. They wanted people. Wanted them alive. Breeding stock, I reckon. Those as can. They ranch us, you know?"

I nodded barely as Siva cracked his watering eyes. "I do."

The old man shuddered, snot bubbling from his ruined nose. I had no kerchief to offer him, and looking round I spied no box in the conference room. Siva continued, "And the things they do to the others . . . the ones that ain't fit to eat. The ones they can't breed . . ."

"What about the bombing, M. Siva?" Valka asked, gently as she could. "What about the siege towers?"

"They weren't no towers," the old man said. "My Uncle Raji, he was in the ODF, used to fix jump ships. Lighters. Used to take me with him. I know my ships, lordship, I do." The tears had come again, and again Siva shook his head, moved his hands to shield his eyes.

"You're sure?" I asked, feeling dread like cold iron clamp round my heart and twist my guts in its fist. "You're sure they were human ships?"

"They were old Manta-IIIs, I'd bet my life on it. All these years . . . I still don't know why. Why would they do it? Why would they rain fire on us?" He let his hands fall, eyes shining. "They were supposed to keep us safe."

"They were," I agreed and placed my own hands on the

table. "Thank you, M. Siva." I looked round again, hoping to find some junior officer or adjutant, but we three were all alone. "Valka, can you go find one of Crim's lieutenants. Any of them will do. I want M. Siva taken to the *Tamerlane* and treated."

She stood, understanding my intentions without having to ask. Siva had been very brave to speak. After all he'd been through, I had just asked him to speak against the lauded ruler of his world. He would not be safe on it anymore. The others would know he had spoken to me, and if the Baroness were indeed guilty of the mass murder Siva had accused her of, then those loyal and devoted to the Baroness would never forgive him, nor would the Baroness herself. He would never find peace on Thagura, not anywhere. He would have to come with us.

"I'll wait with him," I said, and did my best to smile, hollow though the expression was.

CHAPTER 6

OF FLIES AND SPIDERS

PSELDONA AGAIN.

The blackened city stretched away beneath us, a desolation of twisted metal and pale ash. When first we'd swept over that ruin, I'd felt myself sick at heart, thinking of the horrors of the Cielcin, the horrors of our too-long war. That second time, I saw it with new eyes. I spied the greenhouses as we approached, shattered but still standing on the sands below the inselberg crowned by the ruined palace. Peering back, I saw the shapes of the other ships of escort, each carrying half a hundred men. Crim and Bressia and the high officers had remained behind to coordinate relief and mop up any remaining Cielcin at the polar camp. Varro's science team would want to perform forensic work as much as possible, and when that was done, I'd left orders for the site to be annihilated with antimatter charges. Wiped from the map.

No part of it should remain.

"She has to pay," Valka said from the seat across from me in our private language, peering down at Malyan's devastation.

"If she truly is guilty," I agree.

"Truly?" she glared at me with hard eyes. "Do you doubt it? After all we've heard?"

I shook my head. "She must answer for what she's done," I said, casting about the chamber, counting the helmeted heads of my guard. Not a one of them understood Tavrosi Panthai, but I still wished we had no audience for this. It would not do for my men to see us argue, and so I kept my tone as neutral as I could. "If she's guilty, she must go to Marinus. She may face the strategos and Imperial justice."

"Imperial justice?" Valka echoed me again. "Please. She is one of your palatines. She will be ferreted to some prison planet. She won't even have to live her sentence. Your Emperor will put her on ice for a century. Two. Only to have her thawed out again and sold to some Perseid count for her genome. She won't suffer a day in her life."

The venom in her tone shocked me. We had been so long apart—her in fugue while I mingled with the Imperial court—that I had forgotten the intensity of her hatred for our way of life, and of our nobility in particular. She carved some exception for me in her heart, and I supposed that I had thought it a sign that she had tempered in time. Evidently I was wrong, as I could not say that she was wrong.

"You may be right," I said at last.

"I *am* right," she said, crossing her arms over her crash harness. She peered back out the window between us. "How many people do you think were in the city?"

I didn't answer her at once. It was a question we could have answered. I knew there had been forty million on the planet itself, making Thagura far and away one of the largest

QUEEN AMID ASHES

fiefdoms in the Norman Expanse. But in the city itself? It could have been as many as ten million or as little as two. Much of the planet's population was spread across the temperate zones, where the planet's rare water was more common.

How many of them yet remained was hard to say. It would not be until Malyan's people—or whoever replaced them—were able to import relief forces and conduct a new census that we would be able to fully appreciate the cost of the invasion . . . and of the Baroness's reply. I know the answer now. That census was done, years after I departed, conducted by Sir Albert Trask, the man made Imperial proconsul on Thagura after the invasion.

Twenty three million people remained on the planet, barely more than half . . . and there were eight million people in the city when it burned. Eight million people gone in a day. In an instant.

"It doesn't matter," I said at last. It didn't really. "Too many."

"The woman should die for this," Valka said.

Her words tore my attention away from the city beneath us. We had passed back into the shadow of the great Rock, and Vahan's colossus peered in at us. "If she's guilty," I agreed—or thought I did.

"She is guilty," Valka asserted.

Resting my head in my hands, I pressed the heels of my thumbs into my eyes. I had barely slept on the flight down from the pole, and it had taken medication to get me there. The sight I'd seen through the doors of the abattoir would not leave me, nor the mute accusation in the eyes of the heads on the wall. I almost yearned for cryonic fugue again, to sleep between the stars. Half-dead, at least, I'd sleep.

"It hardly matters who wins this damned war," Valka muttered, her bitterness like acid on her tongue. "We're as bad as they are."

"We're not," I said reflexively.

Golden eyes found mine. "How can you say that, even now?"

Perhaps you ask yourself that very question, Reader. Perhaps you sit there and whisper to your pages, asking if I am not the *Sun Eater*? Asking if it was not I who burned the fleet at Gododdin and set fire to that whole world? It was. In the annals of history's greatest killers, Gadar Malyan merits but a chapter, a heading.

I have written several books. I take no joy in it. What I did, I did for all mankind. What Malyan did, she did only for herself. Judge me if you will, but read on, and know that I have asked these questions too, and asked them of myself—and not only myself.

How many years have we added to our wars? How much higher have we piled the corpses? How much deeper are the rivers of blood because of us? Because of our failings? At every turn, with every step, I have found the horrors of the enemy met with horrors of our own. It was us who shot first at Vorgossos, breaking the fragile—and indeed, impossible—dream of peace. It was us who tortured our prisoners on Emesh, was us who fired first at Cressgard and started the war, whatever the official records may say.

We are no angels—nor am I—but neither are we the Cielcin.

"We don't *eat them*," I said in answer.

QUEEN AMID ASHES

When at last we landed and returned along the path Maro led us down to the dungeon and the office of the castellan, it was with another hundred men. The other soldiers—a full chiliad—waited in their ships in a line above the descent to the lower levels and the hidden gate. A new sun was rising over lost Pseldona as we went down, and the dorsal fins of our shuttles rose like black sails against the blushing sky, a solitary line like a row of funeral monuments. Many of the people in Malyan's bunker were only servants; courtiers like the cup-bearer, Ravi Vyasa—not soldiers. We must have outnumbered the Baroness's guards ten to one.

Valka had not liked being left behind a second time, but when I had explained my plan to her, she relented. It would not be easy to extract the woman from her hole without bloodshed, and indeed I half-expected to find the Baroness locked in her paradise, and had ordered a plasma bore and breaching team be deployed from the *Tamerlane* at the earliest opportunity.

So much nearer the equator, the wreck of the battle still smoldered in the skies, its traces visible in the tongues and streaks of acrid black staining the heavens. But where before the effect was strangely beautiful, I could then only think of the smoke of thuribles in Chantry, the scents of frankincense, benzoin, and myrrh.

But Maro's guards did not resist us when we returned. Quite the contrary. We were ushered back down the hidden stair and along the corridors below to the inner door, where Pallino and the men of my guard I'd left behind remained with Maro's men. Between them they had swept the path clean of onlookers.

My lictor greeted me as I rounded the last corner, my helmet again firmly in place. He and my men saluted—Maro's, too—and waited for me to speak. "Is the Baroness still inside?" I asked.

Pallino must have blinked, judging by the pause and the faint shift of his head. "Yes, my lord. She and her captain. Some others. They had word of your return."

I had not ordered word be sent, but I supposed they had yet some access to the surface, some lookouts in bolt-holes throughout the ruined city, and some way of running messages through other doors and tunnels. I paused for only a moment, wondering if I should have sent word, if my silence implied cause for alarm on the Baroness's part. Had I erred?

If I had, it was too late to change. For the plan to work, I needed Malyan to trust me. To come willingly. I had no wish to fight with Captain Maro or his men, or to make of the bunker a charnel house to rival the polar camp. If she was innocent, no harm would be done, and if she was not innocent, then it was better to win the battle before it even began.

"Survivors?" Pallino asked.

"Yes," I answered him. "Not so many as I hoped. But the planet is ours. I spoke with Corvo on the flight back. She's telegraphed the news to Marinus." Conscious of the native audience, I added, "It is a pity the worldship got away. We might have had another of their princes."

Pallino drew aside, fell into step as I approached the door to the paradise. "We may yet, lad," he said, a bit of the old myrmidon friendliness creeping through. "They might not have gone far. If we wounded their ship, may be they wash up in local space."

I clapped the fellow on the shoulder, indicating by that gesture that it was time to move on. He was right, if Prince Muzugara's worldship had been damaged, there was always the chance we might hunt it down, but that was a problem for another day.

The Baroness awaited.

Discreetly as I could, I tapped the chiliarch twice on the shoulder with my fist before pointing at my eyes, making the gesture casual as could be. Pallino and I had been myrmidons in the coliseum together when I was *outcaste,* before I had regained my station. It was an old signal, one of many, one not used by the legions standard, but the sort of thing we relied on in the ring, fighting shoulder to shoulder in ranks, most unlike the shielded hoplites and dragoons of the Imperial service.

Pallino caught the signal plain enough and drew back. *Be ready for action.* There was no time to explain, and always the chance that any subvocal suit communication might be intercepted and overheard. Like as not, the Baroness had neither the means nor the personnel for such intelligence work, certainly not there below ground, but it never hurt to be cautious. I had a hundred and fifty men in the bunker. The Baroness had perhaps a hundred, but they knew the territory, they had the door controls. We were in *her* net, and in *her* power, if she would but use it.

Apparently unawares, the guards opened the gates to the paradise and ushered us inside.

Captain Maro was halfway up the grand staircase from the

pool in the grotto below when we stepped over the threshold, and it took every ounce of my scholiast-trained control not to flinch for my shield catch.

But he raised a hand in greeting. "Lord Marlowe! What news from the north?"

Hooking my thumbs through my belt, I stopped with feet apart, white cape hanging from my elbows. "The camp is liberated, Captain Maro. We've saved several thousand of your people. My people are, as we speak, preparing to relocate them south. There is a settlement near Iudha Oasis apparently unspoiled. My comms officer was in contact with the archon. They are able to take refugees."

Maro touched his brow, heart, and lips, raised his fingers in the sign of the sun. "Mother Earth and God Emperor bless us," he said. "The archon, did you say? The Archon of Iudha? Lady Sirvar?"

The name sounded familiar, and I allowed a short nod.

A smile bright and terribly joyous broke across the bald man's rough face. "O Mother!" The captain put a hand to his brow. "Sirvar Donauri! So the country survived? Thagura is not lost after all!"

It is lost to the dead, I thought, but did not say. Gesturing to my guards, I said, "I am here for your mistress, Captain. We were interrupted before, but Thagura is hers again for true, and needs must that she accompany me to Marinus."

That much had not changed. I thought of Valka's words on the flight down, and wondered what I must say to Titus Hauptmann and the Imperial Viceroy if I failed to bring the Baroness to them. I was a knight of the Royal Victorian Order, one of the Emperor's own, and my victory of Aranata

Otiolo had won me a great deal of latitude, but to execute a Baroness of the Blood Palatine without trial, without Inquisition, without anything but my own judgment would be an overreach. I would suffer for it, and yet Valka was right. Gadar Malyan would find no justice on Marinus, and what she did find would be no justice for her victims.

If they are her victims, whispered a little voice within me.

"To Marinus?" Maro repeated, evidently having forgotten that those had always been my orders. "Is that . . . really necessary? My Lord Marlowe, Thagura has suffered. My lady wishes to remain here. To see to the reconstruction, the future of her people!"

"She did not wish so when I spoke to her before," I said. Gadar Malyan had all but thrown herself at the possibility of travel offworld.

Vahan Maro nodded, but did not step aside. "My lady has been long in thought. It is nine years to Marinus. Even if we were to go and return at once, that would be nearly two decades she would be away from her world, from her people. She must not go! She is needed here! If she must give her report to the Viceroy, let it be by telegraph."

"There will be time for this discussion before we depart," I said, taking one measured step down the stair. "We would not set sail today at any rate. Stand aside, captain. I would discuss these matters with your lady."

Maro hesitated only a second before stepping aside with a muttered, "Yes, of course." He and the two fusiliers who'd hurried up behind him fell into step just before Pallino and myself. We left the bulk of my guard at the base of those stairs—Maro had been too late to keep two dozen men from descending with me—and proceeded as we had done before around the pool.

The Baroness was not where we had last seen her, on the garden terrace overlooking the pool. Maro led us along the marble walkway beneath the nude caryatids, past a pair of round doors in that terrace to a broader door at the far end. The chamber within featured a dining table of pink petrified wood and carpets two inches deep. So lush were the appointments and so deep the silence there that I felt an absurd need for quiet myself, as though I were a rude child again in my father's house. But I caught my reflection in the smoky mirror glass opposite. Where had that rude child gone? In his place a black devil stood armored in Roman fashion, his sculpted armor and serene face mask drinking the light, his white cloak seeming to shimmer in the jewel-light of crystal lamps.

Maro led us through the chamber to a narrow hall that ran along the back wall of the dining chamber and teed off it in the center. We turned down this branch to an armored door at the end—I marked the garret to the right where half a dozen Malyan troopers languored, on-duty but bored. They peered out at me as I passed, curious to see the newcomer.

The captain pressed the door panel, and said, "It's Maro, ma'am. I've brought him."

The panel glowed blue and chimed as the door slid open.

Gadar Malyan sat in a tufted, high-backed chair beside a dormant holograph well, her young companion Ravi not far off. Like any good palatine nobile, she had not seated herself with her back to the door—even a door she controlled. Her hand was on the wood-faced panel built into the chair that had opened the door. She had abandoned her diaphanous robe in favor of a form-fitting gown of Malyan azure. She had pinned up her inky cascade of hair, and the pins that held it glittered silver in the low light.

With a pang and thrill of horror, I realized who she reminded me of. The paracoita Kharn Sagara had sent to me on Vorgossos, the one who had forced herself on me. It was her coloring, the dark hair and pale skin, and the full feminine excess of her figure, nearly spilling from her too-tight dress. She arched an eyebrow, and I reminded myself that the threat here was the same.

She meant to overmaster me, as Sagara had done sending his slave girl to me.

"Lord Marlowe!" she placed her cigarette and its long-stemmed holder on a stand above a crystal ashtray at her elbow. "I feared you would not return!"

"There was never any chance of that, ladyship," I said, putting a hand to my heart in soft salute. "The matter at the pole has been seen to. Thagura is *truly* yours once again."

Gadar Malyan mirrored my gesture, one hand flitting to her heart. "For this you have my gratitude. Will you not remove your helmet, my lord? Ravi, the wine!"

I felt a strong urge to refuse, to order her to come with me at once. But I had to play matters carefully. I had to make her feel secure enough to leave her crypt. And so I raised a hand and keyed the release that opened my helmet like a flower. The segments of the casque broke apart and tucked themselves into the collar. I tapped to loosen the elastic hood and pulled it down, doing my best to smile. "We mustn't stay long," I said, and explained that we had found survivors in the polar camp and meant to relocate them to Iudha in the south. "Your people here should be brought south as well. Pseldona is a ruin. If Thagura is to be rebuilt, it will not be from here."

"Not until relief may be brought from offworld," the Baroness said, brightening as Ravi returned with the wine service. "Will relief be brought from offworld?"

"Eventually," I said, moving to examine a painting on one darkly paneled wall. It showed a team of farmers toiling at their crop, dressed in the homespuns of Sollan peasants. One man wielded a great hand-scythe, blade raised against the sky, while in the distance the huge gray towers of a drydock glimmered about the half-build shape of a starship. There were no such fields on Thagura, and I wondered whence that canvas came. Upon it, the great contradiction of Imperial society glowed in greens and browns and silver: the plebeians at their primitive toil—or so Valka would have it—while we nobiles and soldiers sailed the stars in apparent glory.

What I would not have given then to trade places with the man wielding the scythe. Scion of the Empire I might have been, but as a boy I'd shared Valka's sympathies, her fury at our castes, our hierarchy. Her sense of the injustice of it all. But even in those early days, even in my youth, I had long worn the chains of duty. Of station. That painting was a celebration of our way of life, of the peasant farmer and of the spacefarers who protected him. For it was for them, and for mankind itself that the Empire was ordered. For what is mankind if not the lowest? If not the ordinary women whom we knights and nobiles are born to serve and to defend?

Beneath my white Imperial cloak, I clenched my fists,

thinking of the spider in her chair.

"Lord Marlowe?" Gadar Malyan asked. "Will you not sit a while?"

"I . . ." I turned, eyeing Pallino where he and Maro waiting by the door. The chiliarch adjusted his posture, stood a fraction straighter. "Yes, sorry. I was admiring your painting."

Malyan smiled very prettily. "Ah! Do you like it? It's one of Duri's pastorals. My grandmother was a bit of a collector. She furnished most of this place. We had a genuine Rudas in the palace, but I suppose it is gone now, lost with everything else." She accepted a goblet from her page, and gestured at the lesser armchair positioned at an angle from her own. "It is a pity, my lord, that we could not have met under better circumstances. I feel we have very much in common."

The boy, Ravi, put a glass into my hands as I sat—pausing only so long as it took to brush my cape to one side. "Is that so?"

"Do you not see it?" she asked, putting a hand to her coiffure. "We favor, you and I. A matched set."

I did not point out that where her eyes were black as jet, mine were violet. It would not do to antagonize her. "As you say."

Gadar Malyan lifted the wine to her lips. It was a different vintage than the one we'd shared days earlier, dark almost as her eyes. "I observe," she began with careful grace, "that your paramour is not with you on this occasion. Does that mean you have reconsidered my offer?"

I blinked at her. "You made no offer."

"But I did! You are such a man, my lord. Oblivious, the lot

of you!" she laughed, directed its music toward Ravi, who smiled stiffly. "My marriage offer, Lord Marlowe!"

Again, I blinked at her. Not in surprise, not precisely, but in shock at her plain boldness. I had suspected—and Valka had smelt it light-years away—that the Baroness intended to seduce me. I should have guessed that seduction would go so far as marriage, but I was still unused to my restored place among the palatinate. I had spent more than fifteen years—my entire adult life—outcaste and stripped of rank and inheritance by my father. I had spent those fifteen years as nobody, devoid of status and social worth, and did not expect to find a palatine Baroness throw herself at me. On Emesh, Count Balian Mataro had attempted to secure me as a breeding stud for his family line, for I was a distant cousin of the Emperor, but Malyan had no way of knowing that.

Her motivations were simpler, and confirmed her guilt.

She would have me become her accomplice. She meant for me to fall for her, to drown myself in her. She was counting on love, or simple lust—for power, for station, for herself—to save her. I hardly dared to move. She would not be doing this . . . surely she would not be doing this if she were innocent.

"Don't go all silent on me!" she said, brows contracting. "It is only natural, after all! Thagura must rebuild. I am unwed. You are a knight with no holdings and my hero! What a story it would be."

Something of my hesitation must have shown in my face, for she reached out and gripped my wrist. "You needn't say yes at once. You are a Royal Knight, and have your duties, I know. But think on it." A long-nailed finger traced the full curve of one breast. "You needn't dismiss your girl, either.

QUEEN AMID ASHES

I am unworried about competition. Perhaps she could join us!"

That sent a charge through me, and it took all my composure not to jerk my hand away, to smile my crooked smile and say, "My *girl* might feel differently."

"Does it matter?" she asked, innocent as anything. "She is a tribesman of the Tavrosi clans. You and I are the descendants of kings." She angled her chin as she leaned back, releasing my wrist to take another sip of the dark wine. "Perhaps we may discuss arrangements aboard your ship. We have . . . time before you must go, do we not?"

That gave me the foothold I needed to reply. "Before *we* must go, my lady. Have you forgotten? I am ordered to bring you to Marinus to keep you safe. Thagura will not be stable for some time, and the Viceroy and First Strategos both wish to learn what happened here, and to provide you with an opportunity to coordinate relief efforts with them."

"But I cannot go!" she argued. "I cannot abandon my people, now most of all!"

Rage is blindness, said the part of me that spoke in my old tutor's voice. A muscle twitched in my jaw. Was she serious? Or only afraid of the consequences of putting herself in my power? She meant to manipulate me, that much was clear. Her offering of herself—now and later—could be nothing else. I hid my irritation behind a sip of the dark wine, and it was only after I'd swallowed some that I feared for poison. Too late. But nothing happened, and I broke the brittle silence, saying, "You can do more good for them on Marinus. The Wong-Hopper Consortium has offices on Marinus. You'll need to procure construction crews, housing, agricultural equipment. This you cannot do here.

Your satellite is gone. You have no connection to the wider galaxy. The datanet. Nothing."

This seemed to sway her, and her proud shoulders slumped. "I have a planet," she said. "If Iudha is unspoiled, as you say, we have what we need to rebuild."

"You do not," I said. "You have no military power, no officers. Nearly all your administration was lost in the battle here." Her head began to droop as she listened to me, and she cradled her goblet in jeweled talons. "Has it occurred to you that you may need to *reconquer* this planet, my lady?"

Her head jolted up, and she narrowed her eyes at me, head moving side to side. "What?"

"You misunderstand your situation," I said pointedly, and leaning forward set the wine cup—barely touched—on the table between us. I took a deep breath, recalling what Hauptmann had said in his brief regarding what to expect on the dry world. "The Thagura you knew is gone. Your power is gone. If I were to leave you here, what is to stop anyone—*anyone*—from removing you from what remains of your office? Your captain here?"

I heard rather than saw Maro advance on reflex, but he said nothing.

"You will die here, ladyship," I said, flatly as I was able. "Your cause is not hopeless, but it is hopeless here. Now." I stood, and extended a hand for her to take. "You must have connections. Relatives offworld."

She looked up at me, and for the first time I saw through the veil of coquettish denial she had woven about herself. Her full lips compressed, and there was a glassiness in her eyes I had not seen before. Almost I pitied her, for even if she was guilty of the horrors the Cielcin and survivors alike accused her of committing, she was too a victim. She had lost her world, her home, and everything.

"I have you," she said and, reaching out, seized me by the wrist. "Here. Now. You have an army. Stay then, and help me retake my world. Do not make me go to Marinus."

Her hand trembled where it held me. Her fingers were very cold.

Thinking of all Siva and the others had told me, I asked, "What are you afraid of, my lady?" I knew the answer. It was Imperial justice.

"To lose," she said, nostrils flaring. "My family has ruled this planet for more than four thousand years. Twenty-one generations. If I go . . . I may never return. If Thagura is lost—as you say—the Empire will not fight to reclaim it. In a thousand years, perhaps, some legion will come and take it back, reclaim it for the Emperor . . . but not for Gadar Malyan." She stroked my hand with her thumb, drew it to herself. "Why not claim it for yourself? Become a lord in truth as well as name. Become *Baron* Marlowe. *My* Baron."

Her eyes were shining and she bit her lip—as if thinking. Then, not letting go of my hand, she stood, pivoting so that she stood over me, and as she did I realized that her dress—which had seemed to fit her ample form so snugly—had been held shut only by her sitting down. It unraveled about her, opening like a robe.

And Captain Maro was gone.

For a moment I sat transfixed—as any man would—stunned and scared to move. Gadar Malyan was naked beneath the open dress, unless one counted the sapphire that hung between her breasts, large as any quail's egg. For that bare instant, I was lost, overmastered indeed by the queenly beauty of her, and dared not even to breathe.

Then she bent to kiss me, placed a hand on my face.

I stood roughly, pushed her away and moved to put a space between us with such force that I upset the winecup on the table between our two chairs. The carmine fluid stained the heavy carpet, an unwashable mark.

"My lord!"

"I am not for sale, my lady," I said, taking a half dozen steps to the door. "Not to you . . . or any other woman." A bit of Valka's cruelty—and the old Marlowe family fire—flashed in me, and I said, "Reserve your generosity for a man as desperate as you. Now clothe yourself. We must go."

"You're a brute, do you know?" she said, and I could hear the tears in her eyes before I turned to look back at her where she stood, robe still open to expose the snowy flesh beneath. "What more would you have of me? Shall I bend over here and let you have your way before we go? Will you take all for nothing?" She made to turn, fetched up the hem of her dress.

I snatched her wrist to stop her motion, snarling, "You beclown yourself, ladyship. Tie your dress." I let her hand go. "You talk of nothing," I said. "It is *nothing* that I want, my lady. Of you, and of Thagura. This is not my world, and I . . ." I stopped short, had nearly reached the point of revelation, of stating that I knew what she had done. I still needed her to come quietly, to depart in peace. I'd no desire to fight her men, to spill more human blood upon the sands and so redden that already red world. "Tie your dress. My ship awaits."

CHAPTER 7

JUSTICE

THE CRUSHING SILENCE greeted us with the sunlight. No birds flew or sang in the skies of Thagura, nor was there any grass to stir. The very air was still in the alley and on the street that circled the foot of the Rock.

"Do you have her?" Valka asked, words conveyed through the conduction patch behind my ear.

"We do," I answered shortly, looking back over my shoulder. The Baroness looked utterly out of place in her azure gown and intricately styled hair, as if she were from some other world and not the desert ruin about us—which in a sense she was. Vahan Maro stayed dutifully by her side, face grim. I sensed that he had been behind her sudden desire to remain on the planet, and he was not happy about the way things were developing. Had he pointed out that she was putting herself entirely at our mercy? Had he conspired with her in the bombing? Had it even been his idea?

But I smiled, and pointed around the bend to the stairs and up the wall to where the black line of our shuttles waited.

Another of our *Roc*-class landing frigates had arrived from orbit while we were underground and crouched on the stone above us. "We've not far to go! The frigate will take you and your retinue direct to the *Tamerlane*. She's in low orbit now, straight up! Do you see?" I moved my hand, gesturing to the fuzzy, black knife shape where it scudded across the pale sky. At more than a dozen miles long, the ship appeared the size of an arrowhead at its height of several hundred miles, and its ion engines gleamed dully in the daylight like a fogbound star.

Gadar Malyan advanced, Ravi at her side with a sunshade held over the both of them. The Baroness squinted through small, dark glasses, shrinking from the light. "I see!" she said, casting about nervously like her men. I had to remind myself that she had lived ten years underground, lived in fear of the sky and of the creatures dwelling in it. That experience had surely activated some primitive part of her biology that remembered being small and scurrying in fear of birds. "When will the others be able to make the move to Iudha?"

Falling into step beside her while Pallino led the way, I answered, "Within the week. We will remain in-system long enough to ensure the survivors at the camp and here relocate safely. My people have been in contact with Archon Donauri there. She will join us aboard the *Tamerlane* before long. We will take counsel before we return to Marinus." I winced inwardly at the words leaving my mouth. They were half-lies. Lady Sirvar Donauri *was* expected to join us aboard the *Tamerlane*, but there would be no counsel. Not with the Baroness.

Sensing a shadow at my back, I turned, found Captain

Maro close behind, ever-watchful. His dragoons stayed about us, a line to either side of the Baroness and myself, and behind there marched a ragged assortment of the Baroness's surviving court, those retainers she deemed too important to be separated from her person. She believed they would accompany her to Marinus—and they might yet. They were to be, in truth, witnesses against her. I could not decide if the Baroness were canny enough to surround herself with know-nothings, or foolish enough to keep any confidants close.

We would know soon enough.

We hadn't far to go. My men waited above, ready to surround our column at my mark.

I performed a quick head count. Baroness Malyan had perhaps half a hundred dragoons in her personal guard, and less than half that number in her train. My own men outnumbered her two-to-one, but that was still close enough that a desperate man like Vahan Maro might risk shielded combat if the chips came down.

"What manner of ship is she, Lord Marlowe?" inquired one of the courtiers, a portly man with an absurdly painted face. "Your vessel?"

"She's one of the *Eriels*," I said in answer, turning to face forward again and resume my pace beside Lady Malyan.

The courtier whistled appreciatively. "Red Star didn't make very many of those, did they!"

"Seventeen," I said. "My lord is quite correct." Taking Gadar by the arm, I leaned beneath the damasked sun shade. "Too expensive, you understand. She was a gift from the Emperor for my services."

The Baroness put her arm in mine, forgiving or forgetting

how I'd spurned her in the bunker. "How many crewman does she have?"

"Crewman? About five thousand, full out. But there are ninety thousand men aboard, mostly legionnaires on ice." We had reached the stair by then, the once smooth and polished stone chipped and scarred by the fighting that had come so near the palace. Above and left we would find the square where we first met Captain Maro and the survivors, and beyond that the crumbled road down from the Rock to the shelf where Pseldona lay in ashes.

Not far.

Gadar Malyan's fingers tightened, and leaning in she said, "Then could you not be my army?"

"I have my duties, ladyship," I said, "Even were I to take you up on your generous offer."

"Please," she hissed, and leaning close breathed. "Help me take back my world. You can have me tonight if you would but do this thing."

I did not turn to look at her, but neither did I drop her arm—though every thought of Valka screamed for me to do so. Let her think that I pondered her words as we climbed. We were nearly to the top. "My lady, you dishonor yourself. And me."

She flinched, and drew her arm away.

"We will sail for Marinus," I said.

She did not speak again as we crossed the ruined plaza and exited by the arch to the slope leading back down toward the city. There the pavement cracked and the withered stumps of olive trees rose blackened and gnarled to either side of what had once been a mighty avenue. Our frigate and the line of shuttles waited just below, and I felt my heart beat faster in my chest. We were nearly there. The *Tamerlane* had passed almost to the horizon, its dark shape hurrying about its low orbit. We'd have a few hours before it circumnavigated the globe and was ready for rendezvous.

Time enough, and none at all.

At a sign, my herald sounded his clarion, signaling to the watch below that we had come back. I saw a sentinel on the ramp of the frigate vanish inside, saw Pallino put a hand to his earpiece. He was far enough ahead now that he would not be overheard as Valka or the lieutenant in command of the frigate explained what must be done.

"Are we bound for the frigate?" asked Captain Maro.

"Yes," I said, "she'll take the lot of you." We passed the nearest of the personnel shuttles, and I marked the shuttered ramps, knew that behind each fifty men waited, ready to encircle us.

"So many ships!" remarked the fat lord who had asked after the *Tamerlane*. "You do travel in style, Lord Marlowe!"

"Indeed, Master Pardo!" I said, remembering the fellow's name in a flash. He'd introduced himself as we were preparing to leave the bunkers. He'd been a senior logothete working for the Malyan treasury before the war. "The Baroness's security and yours are of the utmost importance!"

A woman beside Pardo chimed in. "Sweet Mother Earth! I forgot what wind feels like!"

A breeze had chosen that moment to blow up and rake the escarpment, carrying with it the bitter alkalines of the desert and of ash. I felt its dry fingers in my hair, and stopped a moment, transfixed by something that should not have been there. There, at the base of one of the ruined olives, stood a solitary spot of green. A lonely blade of grass, its seed blown there and deposited by just such a wind as blew through our company, bent toward us.

Life had not ended. Not here, not anywhere.

The men manning the shuttle controls chose that moment to drop the ramps. The Baroness had gone on ahead of me, ushered along by her court and Pallino's men, and had reached the base of the frigate's ramp. Men in the ivory plate and red tunics of the Imperial Legions came spilling out, lances flaming and ready as they rushed to encircle the Malyan loyalists. The dragoons scrambled to alertness, hoisting plasma rifles beneath their dun cloaks, drawing in around the Baroness and her people.

It was a miracle no one fired, though many swore and I heard Maro's voice lifted in an oath to blacken the clouds. But it was the fat man, Pardo, who found his wits first. "What is the meaning of this?" he bellowed, looking all round for me. "Lord Marlowe, what is going on?"

My men all stood still as chess pieces, bayonets aimed, muzzles threatening. I had to push through their ranks to reach the front, where a small no-man's-land separated the Malyan island from the sea of red and white about it, clicking my shield into place as I went. The static charge of it prickled my brow, and the small hairs of my neck stood on end. More troopers awaited in the hold of the landed *Roc,* and a junior officer in blacks with the red beret and long coat stood among them, his sidearm drawn.

The Baroness Malyan said nothing. Her eyes were utterly unreadable behind her dark glasses. But she did not act confused. She stood poised as any of my men, not uncomprehending—or so it seemed to me. When I examine my memories of my short time on Thagura, it is to that moment I turn first. I knew then and there that she was guilty. An innocent woman would have shown fear, would have acted lost, overwhelmed. But then and there—for just an instant—I saw the iron in her spine. A moment of defiance and resignation known to many a cornered king throughout the long and bloody march of mankind across the centuries and countless worlds.

"Gadar Malyan, Baroness of Thagura, you are charged with high treason and genocide against the people of Thagura. Surrender, and order your men to stand down, and no harm need come to you or anyone."

She did not, but stood there like a woman weighing her chances. Presently she removed her glasses, eyes shining and narrowed against the light of the sun. "Genocide!" she echoed, forcing incredulity into every syllable. "You cannot think *I* did this! You saw them, did you not? You broke their fleet!" She pointed at the sky. "You said you found survivors at their camp! *Their* camp! You think *I* did this?"

The various courtiers were starting to raise their hands, bunching together to put as much distance between them and the long knives. Maro's men—shielded to the last—kept their rifles level at their shoulders. The captain himself glared at me with eyes like blue fire.

"We are the *victims*, Lord Marlowe! I am the victim here!" Gadar beat her chest. "I am Thagura, and Thagura burned!"

"Order your men to put down their arms!" I said again, not negotiating.

"Rogue!" she hissed, cheeks flaring as she spat the word. "You . . . you cannot do this! I am Baroness of Thagura. This is *my* world! My world!" She jabbed a finger at the ground. "Maro! Kill this man!"

The captain's eyes scanned the crowd taking in the ranks of Red Company legionnaires encircling his charges and his dragoons. He did not fire, but neither did he lower his weapon. "Maro! Anyone!" the Baroness shrilled.

I raised a hand, reminding my people of the need for calm. On the ramp to the frigate, Valka appeared beside the black-clad officer. She caught my eye, but did not speak. Gadar Malyan was the chaotic eye in the center of a storm of utter stillness. "Are you mad?" she asked, jabbing a finger at me. "Arresting a palatine lord on her own world! There'll be hell to pay when we reach Marinus, Marlowe, mark my words! You *dare* talk of treason! *This* is treason!"

"Order your men to lay down their arms, Lady Malyan. Thagura has seen enough violence."

"Put your guns down, all of you!" cried a senior man near Pardo.

Maro and his troopers did not move. Neither did mine.

Stalemate.

"For Earth's sake, ladyship!" exclaimed one of the other women, dropping to her knees. "Tell him the truth!"

"Cynthia!" Malyan's eyes were wide and black as hell, twin spots of ink in broad whiteness. Her nostrils flared, and again she ran the tally, gaze sweeping over her men and mine. One strand of coiling dark hair had come loose from its place and flowed, disheveled, down one side of her perfect face.

QUEEN AMID ASHES

"Please," I said, hands spread on the air before me, as a man placates a wild thing. "Stand your men down."

Her lips trembled, and shook—though whether it was from rage or fear or grief, none but her could say. Her shoulders drooped until she seemed some rag-stuffed effigy propped on a staff. "Lower your weapons," she breathed, voice barely more than a whisper.

Maro and the nearest of her dragoons complied, rifles dropping. One tossed his to the ground, put his hands on his head. When the others did not move as quickly, the Baroness shrilled, "I said lower your weapons, you damn fools!"

Relief played in me, and played out on the faces of the courtiers encircled and on that of Valka and the junior officer. My men did not lower their own lances, but advanced to collect the weapons from the dragoons as they followed the lead of the first man, placing hands on heads and dropping to their knees.

The lieutenant descended the ramp, black coat flapping like wings, and said, "Bind the soldiers and take their weapons."

Pallino relayed the order more loudly, "Double quick, you dogs!"

I crossed the no-man's-land to face Gadar Malyan, who looked up to face me. "I know you ordered your own city burned," I said and, as she opened her mouth, added, "Don't deny it."

She shut her mouth. Was she defeated? Or only afraid?

My gaze flickered to where Valka waited in the *Roc*'s hold. I hoped what we were doing was right. It felt like justice, but what is justice? Only a statue in Chantry, her eyes blinded, a balance in her hands. Thus the cynics would have it. But

I am no cynic. That what is right and just is often difficult to see and more difficult to know does not mean there is nothing just or right in creation, only that we are ourselves inadequate in its pursuit.

"You could have been *Baron*," Malyan said, black eyes filling with tears. It was *almost* a confession, and I think she realized it, for she continued. "This insult will not stand, *my lord*. The Viceroy will hear of your treachery."

"The Viceroy?" I said, and shook my head. "My lady, I serve the Emperor himself, and like the Viceroy, *the Emperor is far away*."

That snatch of the old Mandari proverb struck her as I intended. Her eyes widened, and she realized the folly in her words. The Viceroy was on Marinus, and she would not come to Marinus except through me. *I* was the reigning power on Thagura, not her. I advanced until I was within the reach of her arms. She was almost so tall as me, tall as all palatines were tall, but her posture broke again, and she shrank back. "You and your court will be detained aboard the *Tamerlane* until we have reached our decision." Turning my head, I regarded Captain Maro where he stood not far from his mistress's side. "Your men will be placed in our brig under guard. No harm shall befall any of your people. By the Blood Imperial, I swear it."

She spat at my feet. "What good are your words?"

"Take her away," I said, and stepped back, gesturing that my men might approach and bind her. I brushed past to mount the ramp to the hold.

Then several things happened at once. A bluish light bathed the ramp before me, accompanied by a humming drone. The

QUEEN AMID ASHES

men behind me cursed. One of the courtiers—a woman—screamed, and Valka shouted, "Hadrian! Look out!"

I knew that blue, the color of watered moonlight, and knew as well that constant humming. I twisted aside, pivoting around my right foot like a hinge before leaping back to avoid the slash of Vahan Maro's highmatter blade. The weapon sang through the air, exotic matter rippling like the surface of a pool. The tip whistled past mere microns from my chest. The blow would have severed me clean in half, the blade cutting without resistance.

Time slowed around us, and the fire in Maro's eyes shone cold as distant stars, His jaw was set, and the iron in his heart and hand was a thing terrible to behold. He was a dead man, and he knew it. He only hoped to make me join him in death, in the mad hope that my absence might spare his lady her fate. Wasting no time, Vahan Maro lunged, thrusting out with the blade none of us had known he had. Twisting aside, I snapped my own sword free of its hasp and squeezed the triggers. Liquid metal flowed to its proper state, blade crystallizing in a flash to parry Maro's thrust. The captain recovered speedily, drawing back his sword to aim a cut at my head.

I let him throw it, stepped in with my own parry to stop the captain's blow from carving me in twain. For a moment, we met each other strength for strength, met each other eye to eye. I held my sword in both hands, the blade nearly perpendicular to Maro's own. We stayed there only an instant, each of us mapping the manifold possibilities of the next instant, each anticipating each.

One instant ended, another began.

I arrived in it half a step ahead of my opponent. Before he could move, I brushed his blade down and to one side, and before he could respond I slid in and punched him square in the nose with both hands still on my hilt to stagger him, to stop any remise that might have claimed my life. Maro stumbled back, tried to recover.

Too late.

The highmatter of my blade encountered no obstacle as it bit into Maro's shoulder, nor any as it passed through heart and lung and liver before exiting the other side.

Stunned silence filled the air above the ashen city. No birds sang, and all the men and women seemed not to breathe. The whole thing had happened in less time than it takes to write about it. In seconds. Maro knew he was dead before he fell. You could see it in his eyes, in the soft *oh* his lips made, hardly to be heard. Then his head and right shoulder and the arm with it slid along the fault line and fell. His body fell a moment later, and the stones ran red at my feet.

Gadar Malyan cursed and turned away, shading her eyes. Several of the court women screamed, and Pardo belted an oath. I unkindled my blade and stepped back. Still no one moved. My own troops stood around shocked, realizing each in his time how close I had come to death, and realizing—too—that they had been no use in the critical moment.

Stowing the hilt of my sword back in its hasp, I said, "Take the body away and bury it. Make a cairn if you must." Two of the men nodded. Knowing I must, I stepped over Vahan Maro, taking my cape in one fist to keep it from falling in his blood, and returned to Gadar Malyan, who turned red-eyed to face me. "Those were *your* orders he died on," I said.

QUEEN AMID ASHES

"Tell your men I'll tolerate no more heroics from them."

She shook as she glared at me, and so I took her place, shouting. "Every last one of you, on your knees!"

One by one at first, then five by five, they knelt at last. Two hoplites approached with manacles for the lady then, but I raised a hand to stay them. "That won't be necessary any more, soldier. She's done all the harm she can." The men both stopped, and seeing the pain and fury in Malyan's eyes, I said, "A courtesy for the lady."

CHAPTER 8

THE HANGED MAN

IT WAS COLD aboard the *Tamerlane,* as it almost always is in space. Two days had passed since Lady Malyan's arrest, and still I had hardly slept. The thought of this interview filled me with a sickness and numb dread that forbade sleep. I had meant to speak to the Baroness the day before, but could not bring myself to do it, and so she had waited in the unused cabin I had ordered should serve for her cell.

Two legionnaires in masks and full armor stood guard by the door, each armed only with ceramic blades, for lances and plasma burners were not permitted on ship except at high alert. "Has she given you any trouble?" I asked them, facing the trapezoidal door.

"No, my lord," said the senior of the two men. "Quiet as a lamb. Nothing on camera either, or so Lieutenant Bressia says. She's had watch."

I nodded. "Well, let me in, soldier."

"Aye, sir," the fellow answered, tilting his head. "Shall one of us go in with you? She isn't chained, per your orders."

"That won't be necessary," I said. "She is no danger to me."

"Very good, sir." The man saluted and turned to key the door.

It slid smoothly upward, revealing a small and comfortable cabin of the sort usually set aside for the senior lieutenants, perhaps a dozen feet deep and a little narrower, with the bed built in along the far wall and a notch to the left to fit the sonic shower pod and small commode. There was no decoration, nothing to soften to spartan nature of the polished black metal. A far cry from the lavish chambers beneath the bunkers of Pseldona, that much was certain.

The room had been unoccupied before, untouched since the *Tamerlane* was put into my charge. There weren't even scuff marks and the usual signs of human occupation. It was pristine.

The Baroness lay on the bed, and turned to look at me as I entered, peering out from her curtain of ink-dark hair. That once magnificent style snarled about her lovely face, a disordered chaos, and from the drawn look in her face and the redness in her eyes, I knew she had been crying, knew she had hardly slept.

I pitied her then, as I had not on the planet below. Robbed of her context—taken from her world—it was easier to pity her. Perhaps it was only her dishevelment that drew the feeling from me. Her glamour had been like armor for her, a glamour in the mystic sense, a *seeming* cast over the truth of her. Without her cosmetics and jeweled coiffure, she was still beautiful, but was like a shadow of the Baroness I'd met on the terrace above the pool.

No, I realized. Not a shadow. Here was the woman herself,

QUEEN AMID ASHES

Gadar Malyan in the flesh—shrunken and tired. The shadow had been the Baroness, the gleaming image she'd projected for me. That Baroness had been a mirage, a phantom cast to ensnare me.

A siren, a succubus, and a lie.

The door slid shut behind me. Not wishing to give her the first word and the opportunity to direct our conversation, I said, "There were survivors from Pseldona at the camp."

She sat up then, lips pressed together, but said nothing.

"They must have been taken in that first assault, or so I told myself. Ten years they endured in Cielcin hands. Mother Earth knows what they saw, what they had to do to survive . . ." I let my words trail off, let them hang like smoke upon the air.

Still Malyan said nothing. I hooked my thumbs through my belt. I was not armored, wore only the belted black tunic, dark flared trousers, and polished high boots that were my custom, militaristic but not military. My sword hung from my shield-belt, a comforting weight. I chewed my tongue. "Can you imagine? Of course you can't. You haven't *seen* what they are. The Cielcin, I mean." I hung my head, studied the polished black metal of the floor between our feet. They had given Malyan a soldier's burgundy fatigues to wear, but no shoes, and her painted feet stuck out from the rough leggings like that blade of grass from Thagura's desolation. "I used to think they were like us. Monsters, yes, but monsters such as we. Monsters I could understand—thought I could understand. After all these years, I'm not sure I understand them any better, but I'm sure I understand us men less." I held her gaze. When still she said nothing,

I continued. "There were eight million people in your city, my lady."

"You think I don't know that?" her silence broke like glass, but I marked the delay, the second's hesitation, the second's *contemplation. Calculation.*

She *was* guarding her words, even then.

"These survivors!" I spoke as if she had not, raising my voice to override her. "Told an interesting tale. Perhaps you know it." Then I found I could hold her gaze no more, and turned to one side, paced to the nearby wall and back to the other. At that second wall I stopped, turned my head away. "You see, I was wrong. They were *not* captured in the initial sack—before the burning. At least, not all of them were. They were taken *later,* after the city was destroyed." I paused to study the Baroness's face. Her red eyes were utterly unreadable, her face a study of exhaustion and grief. "Do you know what they told me?"

Still nothing.

"They told me that it was human ships that bombed the city. Your city." I pointed right between her eyes. "Your ships."

"My ships?" the Baroness said, again pausing to find her words. "I . . . don't understand."

"Don't you?" I asked. "That wasn't all they said. They told me the raid sirens did not sound. That they had no warning. There had been warnings of the earlier raids. But none that day. I asked myself how that could be?"

The Baroness sniffed, snarled, "You killed the only man who could still have answered that question days ago."

"Do not hide behind your captain, ladyship," I said. "You

were the one holding his leash. It was your words that caused Captain Maro's death, just as it was your words that burned your city. Your orders." Sensing that I'd pushed too hard on a raw nerve, I drew back a step to put more distance between us, straightened. "You *are* Thagura, you told me. Or are you telling me your own military went rogue? Am I to believe you were a hostage all these years?"

She blinked up at me. It was her only defense. She must have known that. I fancied I could see the gears turning in her head. But she knew as I that had that been her move, the time to make it was days ago, on our first meeting.

Still, she had to try. Looking at some spot on the wall beside my elbow, she said, "I know nothing of war. That was the province of my captains."

"You have played the damsel well, and tried to conceal much by pretending that you are only a woman," I said. "But I do not believe it. Of you, or of any woman." I returned to the center of the room and faced her square on. "Eight million people, Gadar Malyan. How many of them died by your word?"

"They took so many!" she said, gripping the edge of her bed until the mattress squeaked in the confined space. "So many in the first days!"

"That may be so," I said. "But that is not an answer an innocent woman would give."

She seemed to deflate then, to collapse entire, like a fleet of sails tangled on the solar winds. She knew I was right, knew there was no sense in deception. She stayed that way a long time, and I left her alone with her secret thoughts, not speaking. Her black hair hid her face, and seated on the edge of the bed, she appeared shriveled, shrunken by the weight of her life.

"How long did you wait?" I asked at last. "A week? Two?"

Nothing. Again.

"Why did you do it?" I asked. "Why give the order?"

She shook her head, knowing she had already betrayed herself.

"Tell me, Lady Malyan," I said, putting my hands behind my back. I tried to sound kind.

One reddened black eye glowered up at me through hair dark as my own. "We lost our fleet. We had nothing. No defenses. And the Emperor was *far away*." She started shaking, clenched her fists upon her knees. "I had to act."

"And so you massacred your own people?"

"You would rather they end up enslaved to the Cielcin?" She looked me fully in the face then. There was no light in those jet chips she called eyes, none but the reflection of fires only she could see. "We were alone! Defenseless! Without any starships to reply!"

I had to walk away, turned to face the wall, ears pricking for any movement from the Baroness, but there was none. "'The sun is high, and the Emperor is far away'," I parroted, shading my eyes. "You said that before. It's an old Mandari proverb, but it doesn't mean what you think. It doesn't grant you latitude and a long leash. It's a lament. A lament that the Emperor is not nearer his subjects, and better able to defend them from the likes of *you*." For has it not been the case in every age that the greatest ally of the common man has ever been the emperor? The king and his laws against the nobility who ever believes itself above them? The high and the low against the middle?

Malyan scoffed. "You think yourself the only lettered man in the galaxy?" She tossed her raven hair. "I have done *nothing* that others have not done before me, that you would not have done in my place. You know well as I that when the barbarians come calling, you burn your fields to deprive them of food and *pray* they pass on."

My mouth hung open an instant, and for one of the vanishingly few times in my life, I—the son of a poet and student of the scholiasts' tradition—was truly speechless. Valka's words whispered at my shoulder. *We're as bad as they are.* Every cell and synapse wanted to argue with her, but I could never argue with her. Not to her satisfaction.

I never could.

We're as bad as they are.

At length I found my tongue. "Men," I managed, "are not *wheat*."

She held my gaze and did not look away. After another silence, she said, "You're wrong." I opened my mouth both in stunned amazement and to shout, but she plowed ahead, saying, "I have seen what they are. The Cielcin. I know what they're capable of." From the way her voice shook—the audible pathos of it—I knew this, at least, was truth. "They came to my world to *feast*, Lord Marlowe. To carry off my people! Even the children!" Again her shoulders shook, and those red-black eyes fixed on some indeterminate point on the wall behind me. "So do not talk to me of *them*. I did what I had to do to try and stop them. And when I failed . . . I did what I thought was right."

"You admit it?" I asked. "You thought . . ."

But she was not finished, and the fire in her flared hot as any corona. "I thought to deprive the enemy of . . . of fodder!"

"You fool," I said, quietly as I could. "You did not deprive them of a feast, you deprived them of *hope*. The Cielcin travel between the stars for centuries. They don't freeze themselves as we do. They eat what they can raise on their ships; or their slaves; or each other, if they have to. And they *would* have had to. They were starving when they arrived." For a third time, I turned my back. "The ironic thing is, if you had done nothing, they might have had their fill and left sooner. You gave them no choice. Pseldona was their best option, a fifth of the planet lived in that city."

"And I ask you again," she said, "ought I to have let my people suffer?"

"So you committed genocide from an abundance of mercy, is that it?" I snarled, unable to bite back my retort a third time. "Spare me, Lady Malyan! You were afraid! You're still afraid! It's written on your face, plain as anything. You thought that if you burned the city, they might spare you. You and your court of Morlocks underground." My hand moved to my sword hilt, fingers squeaking on the wine Jaddian leather. "Do you deny it?"

"Morlocks?" I could hear the confusion in her voice. But she must have seen my hand on my sword hilt, for she fell silent as a stone. I took my hand away, turned once more to face her.

The Baroness Gadar Malyan had drawn her knees to her chin like a child, and hugged herself, unblinking. In a voice pressed flat and dry as flowers between the pages of a folio, she whispered, "What is to become of me, then? On Marinus?"

QUEEN AMID ASHES

I shook my head. Valka was right. On Marinus, the Viceroy and Lord Hauptmann might find her guilty, but like as not they would sentence her a term on some prison colony, to Belusha or Pagus Minor. It wasn't right, nor could it be made right. Once, I might have balked at the thought of doing what I knew I must, but those who balk at justice and shudder at its retributive nature are fools—as all young men are. Justice, by its very nature, must be retributive. Punishment must follow crime, and cannot precede it. Criminals cannot be brought to justice before their crimes, because before their crimes they are not criminals. Man becomes monstrous by his actions, though the monster dwells in all our hearts, as it dwells in mine. Lurking. Waiting. Biding its time.

None of us is born evil.

Our choices make us so.

"You cannot go to Marinus," I said shortly, knowing what must be done. "We will return to Thagura . . ." I tarried then, tarried because I did not want to say what I must, but I ought to have gone on. For hope, bright and terrible hope, blossomed in the condemned woman, and her eyes cleared for an instant. For just an instant. I shut my own. "You shall die on your own world."

Silence then. Total and absolute.

"I see," she said, and to my astonishment, she did not argue. She did not grovel. She did not beg. She let her knees fall, feet back on the cold, metal floor, and sat square and still. She did not even blink. "I see," she said again, and nodded. Tears shone in her eyes but did not fall. "How?"

"You are palatine," I said in answer. "You'll be beheaded, in the old way."

That answer made the reality more real, and her stunned expression shattered. Her eyes found me then in all the emptiness she perceived, and sharpened to twin points of black. "Who are you to judge me? You are no magister! No praetor of the Chantry!"

I studied her face once more, seeing not the eugenic beauty there, but the stains beneath her eyes, the hollowness in her unpainted cheeks, the pain and horror and care. Earlier I spoke of the plebes, of the survivors from the camp, of all they must have suffered and had to do to survive. Survival makes animals of us all, as it had made one of her.

Animals.

Monsters.

"I am Thagura," I said at last, not really thinking. *And a servant of the Emperor*, I thought. She inhaled sharply, as if slapped, and I amended, "I am all Thagura has."

"Mother Earth rot your bones, Lord Marlowe," she hissed, and spat again between us. "You'll sit here one day. Right here. For just such a sin as mine." She slapped the bed beside her. "I pray you lose everything, too. Your world, your people, that little witch who's wrapped you round her finger. Everything. And I pray you have as self-righteous a judge."

I might have struck her then, and it would have felt like righteousness. But I knew that it was not. She was beaten, and having no venom left to sting, still bit. Having no reply or comfort for her, I could only smile. But it was the broken, crooked smile of House Marlowe, and no comfort at all.

My fist was raised to bang upon the door by the time she called out, "Lord Marlowe!"

I froze. "What?"

QUEEN AMID ASHES

"How did you know? Know that the Cielcin were starving?"

So simple a question at the end of so much talk. I struggled not to laugh, and pounded on the bulkhead all the same. The door slid smoothly up and open an instant later, and the two guards peered in through blank masks. "I asked them," I said shortly. "They told me."

Gadar Malyan *almost* snorted. "And you believed them?"

There was nothing left to say.

CHAPTER 9

THE DEVIL'S LOOKING GLASS

THERE ARE THINGS stronger than our words for them. Have I not said so? Or perhaps I *will* have said so when all is done. In some other place. But it is so, regardless. Time and space. Death. Stone. Sea. Things that are and would be even without us. Things that are in nature and belong to it.

But there are things weaker than our words. Many things. Civilization is one. Civilization is a story we tell, a story in which we are only players, characters on a stage. There are others: history, for example—the field if not the string of incidents itself—would not exist but for our making of it, for history is another story we tell. So too is virtue weaker than we, as are goodness, and beauty, and truth itself.

And justice. Justice perhaps most of all.

Please understand: I do not say that we have invented these things. On the contrary, I believe these things make us, shape us as a narrative shapes its characters. Indeed, I believe these weaker things are higher, deeper than we, and are so made mutable by their hiddenness, their remoteness from us. But we may bend them, or deny them, or negate them, as we may not negate the baser realities of time and space.

I knew what I must do, had set my feet upon the course, but still I did not wish to walk it.

I knew Valka was right this time. Right about Imperial justice. I have said so more than once. There would be no justice for Thagura's murdered millions, not on Marinus, not from Hauptmann or the Viceroy.

But I could not give them justice myself.

Earlier I wrote that justice is punitive. That it must be so to be at all just. Without number are the voices raised throughout time in opposition to this principle, and the ink they have spilled in that opposition might drown the fabled seven seas of Earth. I understand their objections. Those who set their pen against the sword and the gallows and the firing squad did so from an excess of mercy, and mercy is virtuous, if a weaker, higher thing in itself. But justice is a virtue also, and if a man is to rule, it must be with the rod in one hand and the white glove on the other.

Yet still the critics foam, and say that to punish criminals is simple vengeance, and that the agents of justice are butchers little different from the butchers they are ordered to slay.

I say it is not so, though I hear you groan across the countless years.

I am the Sun Eater, you say, and you are right. Malyan murdered millions by fire. I have murdered billions by fire brighter still.

I say to you it is not that there is no justice, only that what justice there is beneath our stars is insufficient. That is why the critics howl, not because they object to the justice of princes, but because they sense the limitations of that justice. No punishment a prince might deal—not even the justice of Caesar—could restore the dead to life. How dare any prince presume to offer justice when he could not restore what was lost!

Oft I think the ancients were wiser than we. They did not put the guilty to the sword out of simple retribution, but to commend their spirits into the hands of whatever power there is or they believed might be higher and deeper than mortal wisdom. By removing the guilty from the world, they blocked whatever future harm such men might cause, yes . . . but more than that, they did so acknowledging the limitations of their own human power to make right whatever wrong the guilty had done in life.

They sent them into the Howling Dark of death to await judgment by the very author of our narrative, sent them to be judged as I have been judged—and will be judged.

As I knew I must send the Baroness Gadar Malyan ere long.

And so I did not sleep, not that night.

CHAPTER 10

...AND THE EMPEROR IS FAR AWAY

DRY AS THAGURA WAS, there were but few clouds in her sky. Perhaps a week had passed since my meeting with the Baroness in her cell, during which time I had met with Lady Donauri, the Archon of Iudha, who had survived the siege. It had taken much to convince her of the truth. Even the Baroness's confession to me seemed not to convince her, there had been such love for Gadar Malyan before. But Thagura was not the same world it had been—would never be the same again, though new life would grow and rebuild.

You can never step in the same river twice, nor upon the same planet. Time, Ever-Fleeting—as I have often reflected—flows in but one direction, and it is not *back*.

At length, Donauri agreed to rule on Thagura in our absence, pending the arrival of Imperial troops from Marinus or elsewhere. Unto her would be given the survivors of Malyan's court, and unto her would fall the decision of what to do with them. Let her sift the lambs from the goats, let her determine who else was guilty, and how. I had a different destiny, would have to answer to Imperial command on Marinus in my time. Standing in the ruined square, I told myself that would not matter, that what I had done was just . . .

. . . and that what I must do there—that day, in that square—must be just, too.

My own men filled the plaza, formed ranks about its perimeter, lances or rifles held at rest. Faceless as they were, I felt myself almost alone in the universe. Two dozen of my officers stood in a line at my left, black-clad in their bridge coats, red berets bent over the left. Crim stood chief among them, wearing his black coat like a cape over his bright Jaddian *dolman* with its belt of throwing knives. Seeing me watching him, he gave a tight nod.

Valka stood to one side of the crowd, protected by my men. She did not see me looking, but looked back to where the shuttle carrying the Baroness circled in its final descent. Seeing it, the gathered Thagurans—survivors from the camp, Siva among them; men and women up from Iudha; and some of the courtiers who had endured in Malyan's bunker. These seemed even more remote to me than the faceless soldiery, almost members of another species.

My men had toiled the previous night to erect something like a scaffold. Thagura had little wood, and so they'd lashed a number of supply crates together to make a kind of stage in the center of the plaza. Their black surfaces gleamed dully in the colorless light, and I could feel the faint heat of them through my boots. The day was warm, was likely to grow warmer, and dressed in my tunic and trousers—without my armor's cooling suite—I experienced Thagura as never before. Dry and hot, the air leeched the moisture from my face, and the wind snapped at my hair.

"Not long now," Pallino said, speaking from my shoulder. "Bressia says they've landed."

I raised a hand for quiet. I did not trust myself to speak.

I had killed before, in battle and in duels, but I had never once performed an execution. Though I had spent the night contemplating the possibility of my own death in the morning, I had never been made to pause and ruminate upon the death of another. Almost I wished to trade places with the Baroness. She at least would not have to live with the consequences of what she had done.

The old systems of democracy and parliament only allowed the cowards to hide. My father's words floated at me from childhood, from another world. Those old systems had killed bloodlessly, painlessly, by bureaucracy, as the kings of the Golden Age killed by their servants. I knew I could not, and touched the hilt of sword where it waited, to reassure myself that it was still there.

At the entrance to the square, Oro sounded his trumpet, a deceptively bright and airy sound. Three long notes he sounded. Three to mark the arrival of the Baroness and her escort.

Oro fell silent as my guards brought her forth. They *had* shackled her for the occasion, and she wore still the burgundy fatigues—without emblem or device—of a common soldier. But her hair was clean again and brushed over one shoulder, running like spilled ink, and her eyes—as dark—were fixed on some point beyond human seeing, somewhere on the Rock above, where the graven images of her ancestors looked down and shouldered the shattered legacy of their house.

We have to show the people we are people, not some abstraction. It was like father stood beside me, a hand on my shoulder. How I'd hated him then. How I understand him now, as I had tried to teach the Baroness.

It is by the sword we rule.

It was by the sword I ruled Thagura then, if only for one more day, would be by the sword that Sirvar Donauri must rule the survivors in Iudha and retake her world, as I had taken it from the Cielcin. It would be a long campaign, but there was order at the end, order and life again. And peace, if not the peace I'd sought as a boy.

Which ancient god was it who said he brought not peace, but the sword?

Is it not oft true that peace comes only after the sword is drawn and bloodied?

So it has been for me.

An eerie silence played over the square as bright-haired Lieutenant Bressia led Gadar Malyan to the platform on which Pallino and I stood. No true silence, for a murmur of dry words floated on the air, carried by the stiff breeze. Though my men all were silent, the Thagurans shifted and whispered, elbowing one another, jostling that each might get a better look at his lord.

"My lady!" one cried aloud, and turning I saw a hand upraised. "Lady Malyan!"

"Lady Malyan!" another shouted, drawing her gaze, too.

"Is it true?" A woman's voice rose up. "Is it true what they say?"

The Baroness did not answer, but turned her face away.

QUEEN AMID ASHES

At a sign from one of the officers, Oro sounded his horn once more, a brief flurry of notes calling for the attention of all gathered. Fresh silence fell, and turning from the Baroness, I raised my voice to be sure all gathered might hear. "In the name of His Imperial Radiance, William XXIII of the Aventine House, Firstborn Son of Earth, I, Hadrian of the House Marlowe-Victorian, a Royal Knight and Servant of our Honorable Caesar, have declared that, for the high crimes of genocide and of treason against sacred humanity, the Lady Gadar Malyan VII, Baroness of Thagura and Archon of Pseldona Prefecture, shall die this day by the sword."

The words belonged to some other man, were spoken in some other voice. A voice that sounded so very like my father's. If I try, I can almost hear it now, can remember the flat echoes rebounding from the crumbling facades of the buildings all around, can feel the uneasy shifting of the crowd.

As in antiquity, the firing squad and the noose were common ways to die. Thus tradition demanded all palatine lords and ladies die by beheading. That same tradition—codified in the Chantry's *Index of Law*—specified that the sword should be not highmatter, but polished zircon, a white ceramic blade lighter than water and sharp almost as highmatter itself. I met a student of the law once who told me that the Chantry Synod had decreed it so because highmatter required no skill to cut, and the death of any great lord should be a ritual undertaken with the utmost care. The carnifex should have been a cathar of the Chantry, a man trained in the arts of death.

But there were no such students in the throng.

"Is it true?" a new voice called out, and I could not find the speaker.

"It isn't right!" another shouted. "You are a knight, and she a lady! By what right do you judge her?"

"By this!" I called in answer, snapping the hilt of my sword free from my belt. I raised the Jaddian weapon high for all to see. "And by her own words! She has confessed her crimes! It was by her command that this city and its millions burned! She sought to save herself, in the hope that by burning Pseldona, she might encourage the enemy to move on! It did not work, and even if it had, it would not have worked for the millions dead here."

The strength of my words seemed to still their objections a moment, and so I pressed on. I did not anticipate a riot, but I needed to keep control of the crowd, and so I moved to the edge of the makeshift platform, sword unkindled in my hand. The wind tousled my hair and my cape and pulled at the red aiguilettes pinned at my shoulder. "The Cielcin are gone. I pray they will not return. But Thagura is yours, is *ours*, is man's once more! You must rebuild your world, but you cannot do so under the command of this!" I pointed at the silent Baroness. "Eight million people lived in this city. *Eight million people*, and she killed them."

So many. So few when measured against the billions my own actions would one day claim.

So very few.

"The sun is high," I almost murmured, and turned to look at Gadar Malyan, "and the Emperor is far away. But I am his servant, and in his name I will not leave this world in the hands of its greatest criminal. My Red Company sails tomorrow, and your world will pass into the stewardship of Lady Donauri, who has safeguarded many among you for so long already." I gestured to the Archon—an older woman with hair like spun steel and a face like old porcelain—who stood impassive. I had shown her Malyan's confession, and she had believed. "We will not return, but the Emperor's justice—which I do here today—*has* returned."

"Is it true, my lady?" a familiar voice cried out then, breaking the stiff silence that followed my pronouncement. "Say it is not true!"

Gadar Malyan bowed her head and did not speak, though we had not gagged her. Turning, I signaled that she should be brought forward to the emptied munitions box my men had erected to form a block. I faced her then, the Baroness bracketed by her two guards. Those black eyes found my face and iced over.

"We have no chanter on our ship," I said, "no priest. But I will have my men light the prayer lanterns for you, ladyship."

Her lips curled. "You pretend to care about my soul? Another courtesy for a lady?"

"Yes," I said. I did not then and do not now believe the Chantry's teachings, but I was not without succor for her in those final moments. "It does not end here, you know?"

"What?"

"There is . . . more. After."

Malyan only blinked at me. Those were early days, and the story of Hadrian the Halfmortal had not yet spread across the galaxy. She did not know it, did not know that I had died and come again. "What are you talking about?"

"Death is not the end, my lady," I said, and found as I spoke the words that I could not explain them. It was a thought my tongue would not obey. And so I swallowed, recalling for myself the Howling Dark beyond death, the warmth and light I'd felt as I journeyed down toward the hidden light at the end. I could not share it with her. It was not mine to share. At length I found my rebel tongue again, and gesturing to the block, I said, "Kneel."

She did not, not at once, but raised her chin, defiant.

I circled round to the side of the makeshift block, giving the nod that brought one of my guardsmen's lances into the back of her knee. She fell gracelessly to the platform. I caught her wince as her knees took the impact, and the lashed crates beneath us shook. She raised her head, faced her people behind the lines of my men. "What I did," she cried aloud, "I did for Thagura!"

"What you did, you did for yourself," I said flatly, and kindled my sword.

The blade shone pale and very fine in the colorless light of that foreign star, too beautiful to be what she was. I raised her then, gesturing with the weapon. "Bow your head."

The Baroness turned to look up at me, eyes hard and wild. "You'll lose everything, too," she said. "One day. You'll have to choose as I did, and when you do, you'll see." She nodded and turned her head away, eyes sliding shut. "I did what I thought was right. You'll do the same, and then you'll be *right here* with me." She squared her shoulders.

Often I have found that God puts truth in the mouths of our enemies, for their words are the only ones we ever truly heed.

"It will be cleaner," I said, not rising to the bait, "if you bow your head."

"Earth and Emperor damn you," she said, and bent her neck.

QUEEN AMID ASHES

I stood over her, my shadow falling across her and the block as the crossing of a moon might blacken a sun. I can say at least I did not hesitate with the eyes of so many on me. I raised my sword and—doing so—blackened her sky forever.

HOUSE MARLOWE OF DELOS:
A BRIEF HISTORY

~~~~~~~~~

THE MARLOWES OF Devil's Rest, the family of the Archons of Meidua Prefecture on the planet Delos—of whom Hadrian Halfmortal was the most renowned—claim descent from the semi-mythical poet Christopher Marlowe of Old Earth's Golden Age. This descent is almost certainly false, as are many and perhaps most of the mythical lineages of the great houses. The scholiasts claim the great poet and playwright died childless, and cite innumerable records dating to the time of the Advent and earlier. Nevertheless, the Archons of Meidua have insisted upon the veracity of their claim, and so great has been their insistence and for so great a period of time, that the myth has become bedrock and a part of Delian culture, such that the natives will oft refer to Christopher as the founder of the house. There are even genealogical records that refer to the central, Delian branch of House Marlowe as *House Marlowe-Christoides*, to distinguish it from the *House Marlowe-Victorian* cadet branch.

The Marlowes have only strengthened their association with the ancient writer with each passing millennium. The devil that adorns their family crest—adopted by Lord Timon I Marlowe early in the tenth millennium—is doubtless drawn from the character of Mephistopheles, the ancient Marlowe's most famous creation[1]. Moreover, it is from another of the poet's ancient plays, *Tamburlaine the Great*, that House Marlowe derived its fateful motto: *The Sword, Our Orator*[2]! Biographers of Lord Hadrian have been quick to note that his famous vessel, the *Eriel*-class battleship *Tamerlane*, derived its name from the titular character of that same play: a fictionalized version of the Golden Age Turkic Emperor Timur the Lame.

The true origins of the family are lost in the deeps of time, though the genetic codices of the Imperial High College allow for broad speculation. Careful analysis of the genomes of Lord Julian Marlowe, first Archon of Meidua, and his son, Lord Lionel, show a strong connection to the so-called *White Victorians*, that is to the descendants of the original English colonists of the planet Avalon, with their blood being almost entirely of that stock. Delian oral tradition goes so far as to

---

[1] It should be noted that there are those among the scholiasts who dispute Christopher Marlowe's invention of the character of Mephistopheles, with some scholars attributing his authorship to von Goethe, and others to the anonymous writer of the *Faustbuch*, a now-lost German text of the middle Golden Age.

[2] Marlowe, Christopher. *Tamburlaine the Great*. (Act I, Sc. 2: 154-156).

HOUSE MARLOWE OF DELOS: A BRIEF HISTORY

claim that there were Marlowes fighting in the army of the God Emperor during the Foundation War, but if records of such generations ever existed they are long since lost.

Genealogists instead trace Lord Julian's bloodline to one Sir Anthony Marlowe, a fixture of the Imperial Court on Avalon during the reign of the Emperors Alexander II and Victor IV, shortly before the dawn of the Kin Wars that brought to an end the Third Chamber of the Aventine House with the reign of George III and his hapless son, Michael III.

Little is known of Sir Anthony Marlowe, save that he married a daughter of Alexander II, Diana, and it is for this reason that his name and house were enrolled in the *Cinnabarad,* the Red Book of Avalon, the first list of the great houses of the Imperium compiled during the reign of the Emperor Sebastian the Great shortly after the ratification of the Great Charters in ISD 1443. It was by virtue of this marriage that Sir Anthony and his descendants were accounted members of the Peerage, and enrolled—however distantly—in the line of succession to the then-young Solar Throne.

Following the Kin Wars and the general crisis of the second millennium, House Marlowe faded into penury and relative obscurity thereby, though Sir Anthony's descendants retained their ranking in the *Cinnabarad,* and throughout the millennia that followed, the Marlowes served as logothetes at the Imperial court, both on Avalon and later on Forum after Emperor Raphael IV relocated the court to the new capital in the sixth millennium. Because of their relatively low status at the dawn of the seventh millennium, House Marlowe was relegated to the newly-formed patrician caste by the *Lex Porphyrogenesis*, decreed by the Emperor Cyrus II in ISD 6112. Contrary to popular belief, the *Lex Porphyrogenesis*—which established the palatine and patrician castes, established the High College, and proscribed the rules for reproduction that have governed the great houses ever since—did not abolish the old ranking system in the *Cinnabarad*. Rather, the old houses of the Red Book were rechristened as members of the gene Constellation Victoria, named for the ancient mother of the Aventine bloodline. Under the *Lex Porphyrogenesis,* House Marlowe remained a cousin of the Imperial blood, albeit one of mere patrician standing and thereby ineligible for the succession, but as the *Lex* also guaranteed there would be no lack of Imperial heirs, the idea of a non-Aventine Emperor became virtually unthinkable, of interest only to academics and to the grand dames of the oldest houses.

For the next thousand years and more, House Marlowe remained of little interest to galactic history. Of mere patrician standing, the family was forced to become one of the *bellatores*[3], the nobiles-of-the-sword, patrician families given wholly over to service in the Imperial Legions. It is in the person of Sir Julian Marlowe, born ISD 7503, that House Marlowe regains any relevancy to the historical record. A veteran of the Second Aurigan War, Sir Julian rose to the rank of commodore in the service of the Viceroy-Duke Tiberius Ormund of Delos. He won a series of victories, most notably in the defense of Delos itself, for which he was promoted to the palatine caste and granted the archonship

---

[3] The Galstani word used in the original text here is *talvarioram*, lit. 'sword fighters.'

HOUSE MARLOWE OF DELOS: A BRIEF HISTORY

of Meidua Prefecture to hold as his demesne in perpetuity, and all his heirs after him.

It was Julian Marlowe who laid the cornerstone of Castle Marlowe, the great redoubt that would one day come to be known as the castle of Devil's Rest, in ISD 7583, shortly after his ascension to the role of Archon. Prior to the arrival of House Marlowe, Meidua had been a fishing hamlet of little import, a small settlement on the eastern coast of the continent of Artemisia, in a region called Ramnaras by the natives: a narrow, green stripe of land between the Redtine Mountains and the Apollan Ocean. Meidua, like all of Ramnaras, the Redtine Mountain region, and the Iramene Desert beyond, had previously been under the direct control of Duke Ormund in the capital at Artemia. In appointing Lord Julian to the role of Archon, Duke Tiberius Ormund organized the region into a new archonal prefecture—a region of some four million square miles.

Meidua Prefecture was—in its inception—sparsely populated. Its principal city was in Aduana in northern Ramnaras, near the Cape of Bronze. Nearly eighty percent of the region's then seven million inhabitants lived in the region of Ramnaras, in the riverlands near the sea. Of the remaining 1.4 million people, nearly all were nomadic herdsmen of the Iramnene minority ethnic group, descendants of the first wave of colonists to arrive on Delos in the fourth millennium ISD. But few settlements existed in the Redtine Mountain region in those early days, and it was early in the reign of Lord Julian that the Museum Catholic settlement at St. Maximus was permitted to break ground in the vale beneath Mount Sarbad. These religious settlers were permitted to found their colony by Lord Julian himself, who received an endowment from the then-ruling pontiff of the so-called Universal Church, Pius XXXIX, which contributed to the construction of Castle Marlowe.

Lord Julian selected Meidua for his capital for its position—on a protected harbor situated on a spur of the eastern coast of Artemisia—as well as for its relative isolation. The northern city of Aduana was by far the larger and more prosperous choice, but it was feared that many of the city's elite were yet loyal to the Aurigan rebels whom Lord Julian and the Duke had opposed in the wars, and so the newly minted archon settled in Meidua, where House Marlowe remained for generations.

Lord Julian invested nearly all the fortune he amassed in the war in public works, and under his rule the city of Meidua was reborn, transformed from a sleepy fishing village to a palatial township. It was in this period that the city obtained the first of its famous white buildings, with marble quarried deep in the Redtine Moutains flown in or brought downriver to furnish the city. By the time of Lord Julian's death in ISD 7811, Meidua had gone from a population of some fifty thousand to a city of more than three million.

His son, Lord Lionel, took the archonal seat from his father, and continued much of Lord Julian's works. It was Lord Lionel Marlowe who raised the sea wall about the citadel of Castle Marlowe, forever proscribing the limits of the castle district against the encroaching city. He also began construction on the city's coliseum and on the Grand Sanctum of the Blessed Victims, which would later serve as the seat of the Priory of Meidua Prefecture. Neither project

HOUSE MARLOWE OF DELOS: A BRIEF HISTORY

was completed in Lord Lionel's lifetime, with the coliseum being finished during the reign of the third archon, Julian II, and the Grand Sanctum not complete until ISD 8815, during the reign of the fifth archon, Nicander I.

The last and greatest of the public works projects that defined the city of Meidua: the great locks that replaced the falls of Ramma in what is now the city's western district, was not completed until the reign of Leona I in the mid-tenth millennium. The locks allowed for river trade to penetrate far up into the Redtine highlands, and would allow for goods—quarried stone and metal ore, originally, and later uranium—to descend through Meidua to the sea.

As has been previously mentioned, it was Lord Timon I who adopted the devil for his sigil early in the tenth millennium. During his reign, House Ormund became embroiled in a *poine* war against the Houses of Kallam and Esselmont, two of Ormund's major vassals. An assassination plot—carried out by an Extrasolarian organization know as the White Eyes—succeeded in deposing Duke Leo V of House Ormund and claimed the lives of his wife, concubines, and four children. With House Ormund extinguished, Lord Timon Marlowe and a coalition of the minor houses of Delos system—among them the Houses Albans, Kephalos, and Orin—formed a navy that besieged House Esselmont's estates on the planet Pelgrave. During the fighting, Lord Timon broke the conventions of the Great Charter by bombing Pelgrave City, earning him the name of *the Devil of Meidua*, forever after to be the appellation of his heirs.

For his war crimes, Lord Timon was imprisoned and almost immediately pardoned by Duke Leo's successor, the

Vicereine-Duchess Anamaria Kephalos, first of Delos's new reigning dynasty. The newly minted Devil still had to face the Inquisition, though his enrollment in the *Cinnabarad* and membership in the Peerage lessened his sentence from execution under the Index to a fine of some twenty billion Imperial marks.

This fine bankrupted House Marlowe, and forced Lord Timon to raise taxes, which in turn forced the guilders to relocate from Meidua Prefecture to more hospitable parts of Delos, leaving the city and its hinterlands crumbling and depopulated. Unashamed of his actions, Lord Timon changed the arms and heraldry of House Marlowe, adopting the black and crimson colors of Lord Hadrian's day and the familiar devil sigil. These replaced the traditional colors and seal: a plumed armet helm above a black shield with five golden bezants. Eager to live up to his newfound reputation, Lord Timon issued the prefecture's first *Enrollment*, forcing all those citizens of Delos that remained in his prefecture into servile status, preventing their freedom of movement and ensuring his tax base. This worked, preventing further flight from Meidua, Aduana, and the other major cities in Ramnaras. For the Iramnene tribes and the men of the mountains, the Enrollment amounted to little. The lives of the herdsmen and farmers were little changed, and not even the completion of the Ramma locks in Meidua by Timon's daughter, Leona—which opened the Redtine river to sea trade all the way to the mountain city of Tarsam—created sufficient cashflow to ameliorate the house's debts.

Lady Leona was forced to sell the House's few great treasures, among them Botticelli's *Birth of Venus,* one of the

HOUSE MARLOWE OF DELOS: A BRIEF HISTORY

rare surviving masterworks of Earth's Golden Age. Despite Leona's best efforts and those of her son, Lord Julian III, Lord Timon's fine strangled them, and for the second time in their history, House Marlowe fell into poverty. Still, they retained their hold over Meidua and the region of Ramnaras, though trouble with the Iramnene tribesmen worsened, with regular bandit raids attacking cargo trains crossing the desert to Artemia and the western provinces.

It fell to Nicander II, the tenth Archon of Meidua, to put down the Iramnene tribes. His rule, from ISD 9951 to ISD 10104, was defined by the so-called Sand Wars, little more than a series of police actions of little interest to galactic history. The end result of these was a pacified desert region and increased ill-feeling between Meidua and the desert.

But it was Anaxander, Nicander II's son and heir, that changed House Marlowe's history—and its fortunes—forever, for it was during his reign that a team of serf miners bound to House Marlowe struck the first major deposit of uranium in the region of the Redtine Mountains. For thousands of years, Delos system had been a hotbed of uranium mining activity, but that activity had always been relegated to the outer system, particularly to the asteroid belt that lay beyond the orbit of the gas giant Omphalos. This mining was ever the province of the Exsul houses, most notably House Orin of Linon, who had ruled that outer moon since the early days of House Ormund.

The discovery of enormous uranium deposits on Delos itself utterly changed the landscape of in-system politics, and catapulted House Marlowe from an impoverished minor house lording over a district of but marginal interest to a position of wealth and influence sufficient on Delos to rival that of House Kephalos itself. Lord Timon's debt was annihilated within a decade of that first strike, and by the end of Anaxander's reign, House Marlowe was granted an exclusive contract to mine all uranium in Delos system, disenfranchising the exsul houses.

This contract—the Purchase of Anaxander—laid the groundwork for later enmity between the Houses Marlowe and Orin, enmity that would come to a head during the reign of Lord Timon IV and that of his son, Lord Aleister.

The early eleventh millennium marked a period of relative peace and incredible prosperity for House Marlowe, as the Purchase of Anaxander allowed them to consolidate their monopoly over all Delian uranium mining. This was accomplished primarily by legal means, although the short-lived Lady Caria Marlowe gained a reputation for her willingness to use assassins against her opponents among the minor houses, for which she was known as the Lady of the Knives. The Delian nobility was unable to prove her guilt in any of the assassinations attributed to her—most notably bombing that led to the death of the Wong-Hopper Consortium Director Qiu Peng-Wheeler, which helped stave off Consortium interest and shored up House Marlowe's control of mining operations in system.

Lady Caria herself fell victim to assassins in ISD 10854[4]. House Prestor, one of the exsul houses disenfranchised by the

---

[4] It was for the Lady Caria that the planet Hesperia was renamed in the late eighteenth millennium, when it became the county seat of the Carian branch of House Marlowe, but that was after the time of Lord Hadrian and so falls outside the scope of this document.

HOUSE MARLOWE OF DELOS: A BRIEF HISTORY

Purchase of Anaxander, was implicated in the bombing that claimed her life. The incident prompted her successor and youngest son, Lord Carian, to declare *poine* against House Prestor. The war lasted 11 years, and was fought—by mutual agreement and the dictates of House Kephalos—entirely in space among the asteroid belt. Dozens of Marlowe mining stations were destroyed in the conflagration. The final battle of the Marlowe-Prestor War was fought at Regus Station in ISD 10865, with House Marlowe the decisive victor. Lord Carian captured the Baronet Marcus Prestor, and forced him and his family to surrender their claims to the moon of Lybia. Lord Prestor and his surviving heirs—save the young Lady Lara, whom Carian married by force—were driven from Delos system and went into exile. They lived with family for a time on Renaissance, but their house was formally disincorporated two generations later, with the Imperial Office denying Lord Marcus II's requests for further heirs.

Lord Carian and Lady Lara—unsurprisingly—had a cold and difficult marriage. Lara Prestor-Marlowe was essentially a hostage all her days. For her, Lord Carian constructed the Dome of Glass in Castle Marlowe, which by then the locals were beginning to call Devil's Rest. It was during Carian's reign that the practice of judging the wood carvings brought to Meidua for Summerfair was begun. Lady Lara had a fondness for the art form, and Lord Carian—ever-hoping to please his captive wife—decreed a prize of one thousand hurasams to the winner of the art contest. This began an annual tradition that his son, Lord Julian IV, continued for the sake of his aging mother, and by the time of Lara Prestor-Marlowe's death in ISD 11117—more than

200 years after the practice was begun—the contest had become a permanent fixture of life in Meidua Prefecture and in Ramnaras especially, where the cedars most beloved of the wood carvers were wont to grow. Artists came from as far as the western Iramnene desert, where the tribes carved colossal images from the great baobabs that grow in the tablelands where the waters of the Esen come down from the far mountains.

The best carvings from each year were collected in the Dome of Glass, and by the end of Lara's life, the place had come to be known as the Dome of Bright Carvings. By Lord Hadrian's day, only the very best of these remained on display for lack of space, with the vast majority of the carvings relegated to climate-controlled vaults in the bunkers beneath Devil's Rest, which were greatly expanded by the Lords Carian and Julian IV, fearing reprisals from the other lesser houses following the exile of House Prestor.

House Marlowe was *not* permitted to annex the moon of Lybia by the Duchess Eleonora Kephalos, and the outer moon instead defaulted to the Duchess herself, and became the primary port of call for the uranium trade, with Mandari and Imperial trading cogs putting in at the outer moon instead of Delos proper. This forced House Marlowe to conduct most of its uranium trade through a Kephalos-controlled port, and ensured the Duchess and her heirs got their share of the revenue from the trade.

With the passing of Lord Carian and Lady Lara, the archonship fell into the hands of Julian IV, the sixteenth Archon of Meidua. With the wealth and security of House Marlowe restored, Julian IV—known confusingly as *The*

HOUSE MARLOWE OF DELOS: A BRIEF HISTORY

Second Julian for his dedication to public works and ushering in a new age of growth and prosperity in Meidua and across the broader prefecture—set about building up the city of Meidua and the palace at Devil's Rest. As has been previously mentioned, it was Julian IV who rebuilt and deepened the extensive bunker network beneath the castle, extending the complex to great bays beneath the Bay of Meidua. Additional bunkers were even dug beneath the city itself, and the city's public transport was redesigned, with underground tramway tunnels expanded and hardened for use as additional bomb shelters. Julian extended the seawall to protect the plains north of the city, allowing from the construction of the Laran Starport, named for his late mother, who was much beloved of the local plebeians.

Such was Julian's peace—and indeed the peace guaranteed by the wars of Lord Carian and Lady Caria—that it endured for the next thousand years, through the reign of Lady Constance Marlowe, whose wife, Lady Seraphine Kephalos-Marlowe, instigated a brief but bloody civil war with the House Burke, the Archons of Euclid Prefecture. The true cause of the war is still a matter of some debate, with some citing issues with trade beyond the Iramnene desert frontier, and others pointing at the personal entanglements of both Lady Constance and Lady Seraphine with Lord Alphonse Burke. Whatever the real reason, the war ended with both Constance and Seraphine dead, killed in a flier bombing in ISD 12388. Their young son, Lord Nathanael Marlowe, inherited the throne. Lord Burke forced a marriage between the young lord and his own daughter, Alpharia. Lord Burke intended to force a union between his house and House

Marlowe, that the uranium mines and mining rights might come under his control.

But Lord Alphonse underestimated his forced son-in-law. Nathanael proved a true descendant of the Lady Caria of the Knives, and more ruthless than his two mothers. He swayed Alpharia against her own father (Lord Alphonse being reputedly none too gentle a parent) and hired a Durantine assassin—one of the legendary *Bloodless*—to slay Lord Burke. With the Archons of Euclid thus destabilized, Nathanael conquered Euclid Prefecture by legal warfare, relying on his scholiasts—not his soldiers—to incorporate Burke lands into his domain. This "purchase" was formally ratified in ISD 12551, with the city of Euclid and all its territories becoming a formal part of Meidua Prefecture. The city remained under Marlowe control until the late fourteenth millennium when—during the reign of Sabine I— it was sold to House Kephalos, along with uranium mining rights to the asteroid belt[5].

As with Lady Caria before him, Lord Nathanael's savvy and ambition and murderous instinct made him many enemies, not only the ill-fated Archons of Euclid. Toward the end of his reign, escalating tensions with the uranium miners in the Redtine mountain region and eastern Iramnene desert led to sabotage and a series of labor strikes that culminated in outright insurgency. These revolutionaries— know as the *xanths* for the yellow radiation suits worn by

---

[5] The full rights to the uranium monopoly lost during the reign of Sabine I would not be restored to House Marlowe until the reign of Timon IV in ISD 15852.

HOUSE MARLOWE OF DELOS: A BRIEF HISTORY

the workers, and called *underminers* by Lord Nathanael himself—bombed the rail lines and the port of Ongrost at the headwaters of the Redtine.

Lord Nathanael himself was killed in a bombing following the attack at the river port, leaving his and Alpharia's son, Benjamin, to inherit. Furious over the death of his father, Benjamin eradicated the *xanths*, capturing their leaders and putting them to the sword. Still more he deported. Those held in serfdom were sold offworld or outsystem, while the freemen were—depending on the severity of their crimes—either imprisoned or driven from Meidua Prefecture.

This had several unfortunate consequences, not least of which was the flight of most skilled labor in the prefecture, particularly among the freemen, though many thousand serfs are said to have smuggled themselves across the Iramnene in this period, fearing reprisal or enslavement from the Archon in Meidua. This emigration of skilled labor, especially in the mining sector, dried up much of House Marlowe's profits, profits which were already eroding thanks to the unwholesome conditions Lord Nathanael and Lady Constance had imposed upon the workers.

Thus the prefecture and House Marlowe fell into an economic depression. Most of what passes for economic activity on *any* planet of the Empire is irrelevant to interstellar commerce. Nearly all of a planet's wealth remains on that planet. It has often been remarked upon that the coined specie of the Imperium—the hurasams, kaspums, and bits that make up the everyday currency of the common man—are arbitrary markers devoid of any value, even chemical value, the cost of gold and silver being relatively low on the interstellar market. Interstellar markets have no use for most agricultural products, as everyone knows, and the petty purchases of local goods and services little serves to enrich the great houses of the Imperium beyond what little revenue may be generated in Imperial Marks.

All of this is to say that without the uranium trade, House Marlowe had nothing to offer the greater galaxy, and was so rendered economically impotent. Due to the peculiarities of the Imperium's two-tiered economy, however, the brunt of this depression fell upon the upper classes, with the patrician families and new-money plutocrats scrambling to invest in surer forms of capital like in-system real estate. But the evaporation of offworld trade froze wealth in the region, and it would be generations—not until well after Lord Benjamin's death—that the pain of the *Xanthous Uprisings* would be forgotten and new laborers could be found to work the mines.

Lord Benjamin Marlowe ruled for more than three hundred years, and even at the end of his reign, it was not uncommon for an old man to warn the blood to be careful. "Lord Ben's coin comes with ropes attached," they'd say. "Not strings."

The fourteenth millennium saw only incremental improvements. Lord Benjamin's daughter, Victoria Marlowe, and her son and grandson—the two Williams—managed to revive the uranium trade, but trouble with the Iramnene natives kept the train lines from running, and House Kephalos showed little interest in assisting their vassal. The tribes were a local problem, and the Vicereine-Duchess in Artemia had offworld matters to attend to. Desperate to regain their place in the sun, Lady Sabine Marlowe sold

HOUSE MARLOWE OF DELOS: A BRIEF HISTORY

a portion of the Purchase of Anaxander to the Mandari corporation Yuen Starcrafts, a starship manufacturer whose fate would become entangled with House Marlowe and Delos system for generations to come. The oligarchs of Yuen Starcrafts purchased the rights to mine Delos's asteroid belt and Oort cloud for uranium deposits for a sum of several trillion marks, with House Marlowe retaining their rights to mine Delos and the rocky planets of the inner system.

While embarrassing on the face of it, this enormous infusion of offworld marks allowed Sabine Marlowe to utterly transform Meidua Prefecture. The sanctum, coliseum, and the great locks were all rebuilt. The streets were paved afresh in the white stone for which the city is so renowned, and construction was begun on the Great Forum—later dubbed the Sabine Forum for the woman who laid its cornerstone.

Revitalized, Meidua began to attract Delian plebes once again, and the increased skill and number of the local labor pool attracted the attention of offworld corporations—including Yuen Starcrafts itself. The Delian chapter of the Imperial Mining Guild increased its presence in Ramnaras, as steadily the genius of Lady Sabine became clear: for thousands of years, it had been suspected that the uranium mines were dry. But fresh veins had been found late in the reign of Lord Nathanael, located by prospectors hoping to restart mining operations once the *Xanths* were put down. With the decline of the region, those veins had never been tapped, but their estimated value exceeded that of the contract Lady Sabine had made with Yuen Starcrafts, and before long House Marlowe was outproducing the Mandari on the fuel market.

House Marlowe's fortunes and reputation were restored.

It was Lady Sabine I who first dreamed of becoming a baronial lord. Under her rule, the incomes of House Marlowe exceeded those of House Kephalos for the first time, and she petitioned the then-ruling Emperor, William XXII, for settlement rights in the Lower Perseus, on the borders of the Small Kingdoms. Her requests were not refused, but they were not answered. Sabine I died believing the Emperor had never seen her petitions, and indeed it may be true. Much has been said elsewhere of the character of William XXII. The man ruled from his harem, it is said, or from the sanguinary field, and had little time for petitions.

But the dream of a planet for House Marlowe had been kindled, and would burn in the heart of every Lord or Lady Marlowe to come—or else would smolder in the back of every mind.

Upon Sabine I's death in ISD 14014, her son Timon III took the throne in Meidua, and continued her building projects, vastly expanding the Laran Starport. Under Lord Timon, the sea wall was extended and extensively rebuilt, following on a catastrophic flood that claimed much of the low town in ISD 14088. It was during this period that Yuen Starcrafts—unable to properly expand into the mining sector in the asteroid belt—sold portions of the territory they had acquired from Sabine to the various exsul houses of the outer system, among them the Orins of Linon.

House Orin was another of Delos System's ancient houses, longer in-system even than the Marlowes, being a fixture of the old Anemas dynasty who ruled before House Ormund and the Aurigan Wars, though they only received the demesne of Linon in ISD 11081. There had been Orins in Delos system

HOUSE MARLOWE OF DELOS: A BRIEF HISTORY

when the planet itself was being terraformed, but they had long fallen from glory and repute. Their holdings on Linon were poor and far from populous, Linon itself being an airless moon orbiting the gas giant Omphalos on the borders of the system's outer asteroid belt. They had made their name and their fortune on the mining and sale of Linon's massive reserves of helium-3 and methane gas, but by the fifteenth millennium, the wells were dry. Their purchase of mining rights from the Mandari allowed them to get back into the map of Delian politics—a house ancient and far more noble than their current circumstances. Like the Marlowes—and unlike House Kephalos and House Ormund before it—House Orin was listed in the *Cinnabarad*, making them blood relatives of the Emperor and members of the Peerage. Despite this kinship, the Lords of House Orin were enflamed with jealousy, having been so long marginalized by the High Court of Delos System[6]. Whilst Timon III ruled, the Orins consolidated power in the system's outer rim, such that by the time Timon III passed away and Lord Lucian took the throne in Meidua, the Orins were accounted the wealthiest and chiefest of the exsul houses, having brought the houses of the moons of Omphalos into alignment. Where before the exsuls had been scattered and prone to infighting, House Orin had organized them into a unified faction—known as the Moonlords—with power sufficient to sway even the Vicereine-Duchess.

Throughout the reign of Lucian Marlowe and of his

---

[6] The High Court here refers to the assembly of all baronial lords and archons (posted and titled) in Delos System.

daughter, Sabine II, the Moonlords grew wealthier and more influential, due in no small part to their closeness with the Mandari who desired Delian uranium to fuel their ships. But House Marlowe also flourished, and grew closer to House Kephalos as a consequence, with both Lord Lucian and Lady Sabine II marrying daughters of the Duchesses of House Kephalos (as would become increasingly common with the latter generations of House Marlowe, culminating in the marriage of Lord Aleister to Lady Liliana).

This realignment of political power in the Delos system created a bipolar political climate, with the Moonlords and the other exsul houses balanced against the Duchess and her retainers, who were almost entirely based on the planet Delos itself, and who—like the lords of House Marlowe, were primarily archons and *not* baronial lords in themselves.

This bipolarity came to a head in the reign of Lord Timon IV, the father of Lord Aleister Marlowe and the grandfather of Lord Hadrian Marlowe, the Sun Eater and the head of the short-lived cadet branch House Marlowe-Victorian. Lord Timon IV inherited a House Marlowe restored nearly to the fullness of its wealth and influence, but his reign would be marked by the greatest change in human civilization since the destruction of Old Earth: The invasion and sack of Cressgard by the Cielcin in ISD 15792.

The first wave of Cielcin invasions triggered changes across the Imperium. The demand for raw materials rose, most especially for uranium. The heavy metal, after all, was and is still used to catalyze fusion reactions for the sublight drives of most starships, and with the Cielcin Wars begun demand reached a historic high.

HOUSE MARLOWE OF DELOS: A BRIEF HISTORY

For Lord Timon, this proved all the opportunity he needed. A shrewd man, Lord Timon, if not without his vices. Over the course of several years, he persuaded the Vicereine-Duchess Maria Kephalos—then in her dotage—to buy back the mining rights Lady Sabine had sold to Yuen Starcrafts, relying on a provision of the contract that permitted the system's ruling lord to do just that at his (or her, as was House Kephalos's custom) discretion. These Maria sold to Lord Timon without hesitation, infuriating the Mandari.

Anticipating this, Timon IV arranged for gifts to be sent to the directors of Yuen Starcrafts, buying their loyalty—or so he thought—with certain choice bits of Delian real estate, slaves, and lesser items. As a part of the deal, Lord Timon arranged for uranium to be sold to the Mandari corporation at a steep discount—at a loss, in fact—which Timon intended to compensate for by raising the price for uranium sold to the Imperial Legions above and beyond the amount expected by the tax levies.

All seemed settled.

But for all his shrewdness, Lord Timon was a man renowned for his vices. Where before the Lords of Devil's Rest had with few exceptions maintained a small harem—three to five women as a rule—Lord Timon extended the count to thirteen, including four homunculi purchased at great cost from the natalists of Sen. It was said that the lord never slept in his own bedchambers, and dwelt not in the Great Keep, but in the Rose Tower overlooking the sea, attended by his slave women.

This proclivity proved his undoing.

Apparently grateful for the gifts they had received, the

directors of Yuen Starcrafts gave Lord Timon a gift of their own: a homunculus slave girl, dark of skin and white of hair. Stories say the girl's name was Syanna, and that Lord Timon took to her at once—as he was meant to. To all appearances she was everything Lord Timon might desire, sensuous, obedient, and demure . . . But Syanna had not been crafted by the men of Sen, or any of the approved natalist companies in the galaxy, but by the Extrasolarians. Embedded in Syanna's unconscious was a *daimon,* a *script*—or so the Extrasolarians call it. Triggered by her own orgasm, a script written to turn her into a killer.

Lord Timon never saw it coming. He died abed, strangled by his new favorite concubine.

The girl herself didn't even know she'd done it. The servants found her in bed the next morning, fast asleep.

The death of Lord Timon and the humiliation of House Marlowe brought Lord Aleister to the throne. His first act was to order the execution of the woman, Syanna. Reports on this incident differ, with some accounts saying the young lord—then a man of merely twenty-seven standard years—killed the homunculus himself, beheading her with the White Sword. Others say he ordered his headsman to perform the act, or that the Chantry did it for him. Whichever is true, the event was carried out privately, and despite young Aleister's attempts at containment, the story of Lord Timon's death and humiliation got out.

Shortly before these events, the Duchess Elmira Kephalos had been summoned to Forum to attend the young Emperor William XXIII, who was but newly come into his inheritance. In her absence, Duchess Elmira had appointed

HOUSE MARLOWE OF DELOS: A BRIEF HISTORY

Lord Timon executor of her estate, the Duke in all but name. His sudden death at the hands of the Mandari created a power vacuum and instability in Delos system—one that might have spelled the end of the Kephalos dynasty—were it not for Lord Aleister.

Led by House Orin, the Moonlords formed a coalition armada and went to war with the archons of Delos and the inner system, hoping to seize the central planet and House Kephalos's assets for themselves with Mandari support. Lord Thaddeus Orin, Baron of Linon, first sought to claim that he should rule as executor, being the senior-most of the Moonlords. But young Aleister insisted that his father's rights and privileges were his, and the archons of Delos—eager to keep power in their own hands—backed the young lord's claims. It is likely the archons of Delos believed the young Marlowe, barely more than an ephebe, would be amenable to their control. But young Aleister quickly asserted his rights and privileges as Lord Executor of Delos, and assembled an armada to blockade the planet and keep the Orin coalition from landing on Delos proper.

The bulk of the fighting occurred in the asteroid belt. Angered by Marlowe's blockade and general obstinacy, the Moonlords seized House Marlowe's mining outposts beyond the orbit of the gas giant, Omphalos, executing the soldiers of the various station garrisons and pressing the workers to labor for themselves.

The conflict culminated in ISD 15863—two years later—with the Battle of Linon. Lord Aleister Marlowe, acting as the head of the Delian nobiles, took a fleet to Linon and bombarded the palace of House Orin at Last Watch.

Linon had no atmosphere of its own, and the palace—while mostly subterranean—was dominated by a series of great domes under the open sky. On Aleister Marlowe's orders, these were shot open, and sapping teams were sent in to drill holes level by level until all the air was drained from the palace. Baron Thaddeus Orin and his entire family died slow deaths by decompression as the winds leeched out of the palace at Last Watch.

Like his ancestor, Lord Timon I, Aleister Marlowe had extinguished a nobile house. Unlike his ancestor, Lord Timon I, Aleister Marlowe was praised for it. Praised, and feared. He had not compromised, not parleyed. He had not accepted the Baron's surrender. Aleister Marlowe had made an example of the rebel Baron, and in so doing had broken the Moonlords' coalition for good and all. Yuen Starcrafts was banished from Delos system by his decree, and the other exsul houses were forced to pay damages. Several of them pressed suit, appealing to the Emperor, but from Forum no answer came, nor any Inquisition. Lord Timon I had been sanctioned for violating the rules of *poine* warfare, but the Orin rebellion was no formal vendetta. Thaddeus Orin had raised his hand against a vicereine of the Emperor, had hoped that by stealing the throne of Delos he might beg forgiveness victorious, suffer a penalty and emerge the Duke and Viceroy himself.

He had failed.

There were many who thought that Lord Aleister might press his advantage, seize a daughter of the duchess for his own and claim the throne of Delos. But Lord Aleister did no such thing. Kephalos soldiers had provided much of the

HOUSE MARLOWE OF DELOS: A BRIEF HISTORY

force he'd brought to bear on Linon, and while he might have claimed the throne in Artemia, he could never have held it. Knowing this, and desiring not the throne of Delos in any case, Lord Aleister surrendered the executorship when Lady Elmira returned, and lay the bodies of House Orin before her seat upon her return. As Lord Timon I had become *the Devil of Meidua*, so Lord Aleister earned his name: the Butcher of Linon, though there were many in Meidua and Artemia alike who whispered that *surgeon* was more apt.

What followed then for Delos system was an uneasy bipolarity. Lady Elmira ruled in name, but such was the strength of Lord Aleister's reputation and the wealth of his house—now returned to its traditional monopoly over the uranium trade in truth as well as name—that Lord Aleister became nearly the Duchess's equal in terms of real power, and often the two would consult on matters of state, and rule Delos system as co-lords.

In due time, Aleister Marlowe married Liliana Kephalos, the youngest of Elmira's daughters, though it was said he did not love her, nor she him. But such are many palatine marriages, and in time children came, and it was their children that would change the trajectory of House Marlowe forever.

Sensing that political tensions in Delos system were tightening about his house, Lord Aleister became obsessed with earning a title on some new world. Biographers of the Butcher of Linon suspect that he feared what must follow after the passing of Lady Elmira. The uneasy equilibrium that characterized his co-rule with the Duchess depended upon their personal relationship, and that would not last forever.

The exsul houses remained, a looming threat, and there were factions among Elmira's own advisors who misliked the sway the Lords of Meidua had over their Duchess, and Elmira herself remained the only check against them.

   The desire of House Marlowe—born during the reign of Lady Sabine—reached a positive fever in Lord Aleister. The pursuit consumed him, fearing for the security of his house. While much has been made of the life and character of Hadrian, his eldest son, it is evident from the Sun Eater's own writings that he remained more or less oblivious to the precarious political position of his family. This is no surprise. Lord Hadrian fled his family and his homeworld in ISD 16136 at the tender age of nineteen standard, and is widely believed to have never returned. His own writings suggest an overwhelming contempt for the all-consuming nature of his father's political vision, though biographers of the so-called Sun Eater are quick to note this trait of the father in the son. Regardless, it is certainly the case that Lord Hadrian simply did not spend enough of his life on Delos to appreciate the balance of power there, or spend enough time with his father. For his abandonment of his house and homeworld, Lord Hadrian was attainted and rendered *outcaste* by a Writ of Disavowal declared by Lord Aleister, stripping the son of all rights and titles derived from the family name. By that time, Lord Aleister had already replaced his itinerant eldest son, having petitioned the High College for a daughter, Lady Sabine.

   The brief *poine* war waged by the Lady Lyra Orin-Natali against House Marlowe in ISD 16170 is illustrative of the family's increased danger. The mother of the late Baron

HOUSE MARLOWE OF DELOS: A BRIEF HISTORY

Thaddeus, Lady Lyra attempted to murder Lord Crispin and his younger sister, and so avenge her murdered family. Her plot might have succeeded, were it not for the support of the Museum Catholic population in the Redtine Mountains, who remained close with the archons of Meidua ever after, with the Albé family serving in the personal retinue of Lord Crispin throughout his life.

  Lord Hadrian's impact upon the broader galactic stage is elsewhere recorded. For the purposes of this account, his conduct in the Cielcin Wars saw him readmitted to the palatine caste following his father's Writ of Disavowal, and re-enrolled in the *Lex Porphyrogenesis* and in the *Cinnabarad* as the founding (and to date, only) member of the House Marlowe-Victorian. While not technically a cadet branch due to the circumstances of its founding—meaning Lord Hadrian's prior *outcaste* status—House Marlowe-Victorian was legally distinct from the Delian branch, and remained so until it died with Lord Hadrian after the Battle of Gododdin. Hadrian Marlowe kept the black and red house colors that had been the emblems of his father's house since the reign of Lord Timon I, but adopted his own seal: the pentacle and pitchfork and homage to the devil that still flies above Devil's Rest. That sigil originated as the emblem of the Meidua Red Company, a false front mercenary outfit created by Lord Hadrian during the Cielcin Wars. When the Red Company was formally invested by the Emperor—becoming the Imperial Red Company after the first Battle of Vorgossos, in which Lord Hadrian slew the Cielcin chieftain Aranata Otiolo, the pitchfork and pentacle became the official emblem of the House Marlowe-Victorian.

A third branch of the family, the House Marlowe-Carian, came to rule the planet Caria in the Outer Perseus late in the eighteenth millennium, with Lord Aleister's daughter, Sabine, becoming first Countess of Caria. In her, the dream of her namesake was achieved, and House Marlowe—that ancient house of the *Cinnabarad,* long toiling in obscurity as a mere landed archonal family—achieved baronial lordship.

Lord Crispin inherited the throne on Delos in ISD 17178. Lord Aleister—having ruled for more than a thousand standard years, his life extended beyond even palatine limits by his frequent journeys to the Imperial Court on Avalon, to Consortium headquarters on Arcturus Station, and to the Outer Perseus in his quest to buy the title to what would become the planet Caria. His son, Lord Crispin, inherited Devil's Rest and role of Archon, and rules there to this day, overshadowed by his sister, the Countess of Caria, and his brother, Lord Hadrian…the Sun Eater of legend.

THE ARCHONS OF MEIDUA PREFECTURE

BETWEEN THE TIME of its formal constitution in ISD 7583 and the birth of Lord Hadrian, Meidua Prefecture had thirty-two landed archons. The position is heritable because of House Marlowe's status as a member of the Peerage and its enrollment in the *Cinnabarad*. The family may not be stripped of its titles without either the intervention of the Chantry's Inquisition or the Emperor himself.

CHRISTOPHER RUOCCHIO

The Lords of Devil's Rest and Archons of Meidua are as follows:

	THE LORDS OF DEVIL'S REST	
1	LORD JULIAN I	7583 – 7811
2	LORD LIONEL	7811 – 8078
3	LORD JULIAN II	8078 – 8445
4	LADY ALESSANDRA	8445 – 8602
5	LORD NICANDER I	8602 – 8889
6	LORD PHILIP	8889 – 9127
7	LORD TIMON I	9127 – 9407
8	LADY LEONA I	9407 – 9712
9	LORD JULIAN III	9712 – 9951
10	LORD NICANDER II	9951 – 10104
11	LORD ANAXANDER	10104 – 10391
12	LORD TIMON II	10391 – 10532
13	LADY CASSANDRA I	10532 – 10783
14	LADY CARIA	10783 – 10854
15	LORD CARIAN	10854 – 11008
16	LORD JULIAN IV	11008 – 11344
17	LADY CASSANDRA II	11344 – 11727
18	LADY LEONA II	11727 – 11991
19	LORD LEONTES	11991 – 12176
20	LADY CONSTANCE	12176 – 12388
21	LORD NATHANAEL	12388 – 12562
22	LORD BENJAMIN	12562 – 12913
23	LADY VICTORIA	12913 – 13222
24	LORD WILLIAM I	13222 – 13487
25	LORD WILLIAM II	13487 – 13751
26	LADY SABINE I	13751 – 14014
27	LORD TIMON III	14014 – 14556
28	LORD LUCIAN	14556 – 14988
29	LADY SABINE II	14988 – 15307
30	LORD NICANDER III	15307 – 15654
31	LORD TIMON IV	15654 – 15861
32	LORD ALEISTER	15861 – 17178
33	LORD CRISPIN	17178 – PRESENT

Printed in Great Britain
by Amazon